daddy says

daddy says

Ntozake Shange

Simon & Schuster Books for Young Readers
NEW YORK   LONDON   TORONTO   SYDNEY   SINGAPORE

SIMON & SCHUSTER BOOKS FOR YOUNG READERS
An imprint of Simon & Schuster Children's Publishing Division
1230 Avenue of the Americas, New York, New York 10020

SIMON & SCHUSTER BOOKS FOR YOUNG READERS is a trademark of Simon & Schuster.
Book design by Russell Gordon
The text for this book was set in Bookman Old Style.
Manufactured in the United States of America
2 4 6 8 10 9 7 5 3 1
Library of Congress Cataloging-in-Publication Data
Shange, Ntozake.
Daddy says / Ntozake Shange.
p. cm.
Summary: Twelve-year-old Lucie-Marie and her older sister Annie Sharon attempt to deal with the death of their mother in a rodeo accident, while hoping to follow in her footsteps as championship riders.
ISBN 0-689-83081-5
[1. Death—Fiction. 2. Rodeos—Fiction. 3. Mothers and daughters—Fiction. 4. Sex role—Fiction. 5. African Americans—Fiction. 6. Texas—Fiction.] I. Title.
PZ7.S52835 Dad 2003
[Fic]—dc21   2002005077

This work is based upon the play *Daddy Says*, published in 1989 in *New Plays for the Black Theatre,* edited by Woodie King Jr., Third World Press.

To my mother, Eloise, for her courage and nurturing. Much love, Ntozake

I want to thank my agent, Jennie Dunham, for her patience and enthusiasm. And thanks to Tim Seldes for his support. I'd like to acknowledge the painstaking and wonderful work of my editor, David Gale, and Ellie Bisker for keeping everything in order. I must thank Bettye Stroud for her meticulous work in preparing this manuscript. I want to thank my horse trainers in Houston, Melvin Glover and Al Semple, for encouraging me to run barrels at the age of thirty-five against fourteen- and fifteen-year-olds. And I want to extend great appreciation to Molly Stevenson of the American Cowboy Museum for including me in the rodeo family circuit and the great trail rides that I enjoyed so much in Texas. I'd like to thank the people of Texas for sustaining our culture amid encroaching modernization. I have to thank my daughter, Savannah, who in her enthusiasm to be like Mommy, rode a sheep.

chapter 1

Lucie-Marie held the rope loosely in her hands, trying to make her lasso feel like an extension of her body. She aimed for the bedpost, imagining the post as a frisky young calf. She missed. Lucie-Marie dragged the rope back along the floor to try again.

Late-afternoon sunlight streamed through a window, bright orange and lavender, as the twelve-year-old did her best to snare the bedpost. Long shadows and humming cicadas held the small East Texas ranch house hostage as the summer day neared its end. The rope disappeared into the reflected colors of the sunset, missed the post, and fell to the floor.

Lucie-Marie pulled the rope back and fastened her determined fingers around it again. This time, for sure, she would settle the noose around the bedpost and prove to her older sister, Annie Sharon, she was ready for some serious calf-roping. But before she could get her fingers set just right, Annie Sharon snatched the rope away. With one swift movement, she lassoed the elusive bedpost.

"What'd ya do that for?" Lucie-Marie shouted. "I was gonna get that one. You never give me a chance to do anythin'!"

"How do you expect me to stand by and do nothin' when I taught you everythin' you sposed to know, and still you can't get the hang of it? Now, come over here, and I'll show you one more time." Annie Sharon shoved Lucie-Marie to a different spot in their bedroom, a different angle from the bedpost. She situated her sister's fingers on the rope so it would glide through its loop without a hitch.

This time when Lucie-Marie twirled her rope, no funny-looking shapes sailed through the air. With one throw of Lucie-Marie's arm, she snared the bedpost as she hoped to snare calves at future rodeos she competed in.

"There now," Annie Sharon said. She tossed her head to one side, her ponytail swinging back and forth. She jammed her hands into the pockets of her jeans, and stood waiting for Lucie-Marie to thank her.

"Well, I'm gonna do it again and again till I make Mama proud of me. You know, this is the anniversary of the day she died. I gotta do somethin' to make her proud. She never got a chance to see me rope anythin'. When Mama died, I was only old enough to sit on the back of a sheep, makin' believe it was a real horse."

"Don't you talk about Mama no more, you hear? I don't wanna hear any more about her."

"But, Annie Sharon, she was a champion roper, a tie-down roper, and a bronc buster. Plus, she could race barrels better than anybody. Why can't I talk about her? Twanda Rochelle Johnson-Brown was my mama, and I'm proud of it. Why, by the time she was your age, she could win anythin'. Now, why can't we talk about that?"

"I say let the past be the past."

"Well, that's not sayin' much, considerin' that ever since you could crawl, walk, or talk, it was Mama who had you on the back of a horse. You ignore Mama's guidin' you and make yourself into some kinda newborn heifer. Maybe I should rope you, since you came into this world knowin' everythin' there is to know."

Annie Sharon's jaws tightened, and her hands closed into fists. "Look, I told you, leave Mama out of this talk about the rodeo. I don't want to talk about her at all. Ever!"

"Why not? She's the only mama we got." Lucie-Marie pushed her braids back onto her shoulders.

"The only mama we had, dummy."

"Don't call me 'dummy.' I'm just two years younger than you, is all. 'Sides, you ain't but fourteen." Lucie-Marie's voice dropped almost to a whisper. "I'd give anythin' to know what all Mama taught you."

"Well, you're too late for that. No more of this 'Mama' talk, and I mean it."

"I'm gonna tell Daddy what you did to me, takin' my rope away, and I'm just learnin' how to use it."

Lucie-Marie stomped out to the living room and eased herself down to the braided rug on the floor. Her eyes roved across the many championship belts and trophies won by her mother during Twanda's short life. A story lurked behind every one of her championships. Sometimes Tie-Down, the girls' father, talked about the wild horses Mama broke in. And sometimes he just wouldn't. Lucie-Marie felt cheated because of the way her daddy and her sister kept secret all of their memories of her mother. They treated her like she wasn't entitled to know her mama's challenges and triumphs. Twanda worked the rodeo circuit from Muskogee, Oklahoma, to Midnight, Mississippi. All Lucie-Marie knew was that her mama placed first in more events than any other female on the rodeo circuit, and especially in the events usually reserved for men only. Why did they shut her out?

Lucie-Marie decided not to pay any attention to her sister. She got up and walked over to the shelf above the fireplace. She took down one of her mother's championship belts and fastened it about her waist, ready to go back to her practice of roping the bedpost. The truth of the matter was that her father, Tie-Down, never let her near a real herd of cattle or their calves. Too dangerous for such a little cowgirl, he said. But she took joy in the knowledge that one of these days she'd be old enough to help out like her sister. She knew, of course, that Annie Sharon did not take as much joy in the life they lived as she did. It seemed to Lucie-Marie that Annie Sharon thought of every wild and out-of-control creature as the horse that killed their mother.

"Aw, c'mon, Annie Sharon. Let's put Mama's belts on and go out to the stables. We'll get us some horses and show the world, especially Daddy, that we're the unmistakable daughters of a championship mother. That we can do anythin' she could, 'cause she rides with us. What d'you say? I think it's a grand idea myself. We'll show the world we're made of the same stuff as our mother."

"Lucie, you forget. I got my own medals and trophies. I don't need to live through the success of a ghost. Besides, I've tol' you a dozen times I don't wanna talk about Mama, ever."

"Why do you want to be like that, Annie Sharon? It's only natural for a girl to want to talk about her mama. What's the matter with you?" Lucie-Marie fastened on another of Twanda's belts.

"Goodness gracious, Lucie-Marie, do I have to spell it out for you? Mama died 'cause she set more store in chasing wild horses and bulls than she did in taking care of us. Who else's mama do you know that risks her life every Friday and Saturday, chasin' horses and steers instead of seein' to her own children, her daughters, specifically you and me? And you were just outta your trainin' pants, could hardly run, let alone understand why your mama was gone forever. I don't think she was a good mother."

"Well, I don't care what you say. I'm gonna be just like Mama and win, season after season and year after year. Folks are gonna remember me, Lucie-Marie Johnson-Brown, the gal who wins, just like her mother did. So there!"

By this time Lucie-Marie's hips hung heavy with as many of Twanda's belts as she could manage to strap on. She took down a trophy from the All-Women's Rodeo. "See? All of these say: 'Twanda Rochelle Johnson-Brown.' That's *my* mama."

Annie Sharon sat down, hard, in a rocking chair. Underneath her bangs, her dark eyes glared at her younger sister. She shook her head.

"Annie Sharon, why you always gotta be so evil?" Lucie-Marie started to unbuckle some of the belts she had decorated herself with, but she stopped when she seemed to think of something of immediate urgency. "You know what Lincoln Maceo told me?"

"Nope."

"He says he knows who's been sendin' me those love notes in Mrs. Walker's class."

"He does?" Annie Sharon asked.

"It's him, himself. Can you imagine I might one day marry Lincoln Maceo?"

"Marry with Lincoln Maceo? He looks like a skinny scarecrow. Plus, you're three inches taller than him. How's that gonna look?"

"Well, I tol' him he'd have to come ask Daddy for my hand in marriage." Lucie-Marie giggled and covered her face with her hands.

"Lucie, you've got plenty of time to think about growing up and getting married," Annie Sharon said.

"I can marry Lincoln Maceo if I want to," Lucie-Marie snapped. "He said he'd wait for me forever. Or, I could even marry Jerome Golightly, if I wanted."

Amused by her sister's attitude, Annie Sharon said softly, "You're too young to be thinkin' about boys, much less about marryin' them." She laughed. "Especially not Jerome. He's got a million girlfriends."

Surprised, Lucie-Marie fiddled with her braids. Her eyes downcast with embarrassment, she said, "I haven't figured it all out yet, but there's gotta be a way. I'd love to ask Daddy, but I don't think I will. He's so good with romance, though. Remember all those stories he tol' us about him and Mama? That was romantic."

Lucie-Marie had fired up thoughts of their mother that proved troubling to Annie Sharon. Here stood Lucie-Marie, who could barely remember their mother, parading around in all of this rodeo regalia as if that could bring their mother closer. Plus, she managed to conjure up memories of the relationship between Tie-Down and Twanda that she was not even privy to. It was best to forget everything, Annie Sharon thought: the sound of her mother's voice, her smell, the way her hands fit over your fingers. It was best to forget. Leave the dead in peace. Leave it all be. Lucie-Marie broke into her thoughts.

"Maybe I'll marry Jerome," Lucie-Marie day-dreamed out loud. "We could have a whole passel of children. I think I'll have six, three girls and three boys. Can you think of any names?"

Annie Sharon rolled her eyes at her little sister and dropped her head into her hands. "How're you gonna marry Jerome, if you think you're goin' with Lincoln Maceo?"

"Oh, stop makin' things so complicated. This is for when I grow up. Not now."

"Oh, I see. Well, let's pick some names when you grow up."

"We can do it now," Lucie-Marie said. "First, let's do the boys. Boys' names gotta fit their looks and their personalities."

"Not always. You know that cowgirl, Mavis? Her boy ain't pretty enough to be named Duke."

"Yeah." Lucie-Marie giggled. "He looks more like a Sam."

"Don't say that to Mavis. She thinks that child is a god or somethin'."

"Well, he ain't."

"I was thinkin' Daddy looks like his name. Tie-Down. He looks like a champion," Annie Sharon said.

"Oh, I think it's even better than that. I think he looks like he has rodeo in his blood. He sho' don't look like an 'Elmer' or a 'Winthrop.'"

"Who d'you know named Winthrop?"

Lucie-Marie frowned. "Oh, I heard it on television, that's where. It was the name of somebody with lots of money."

Annie Sharon's mind wandered from her sister's fantasies to their real world. "You know what?"

"No, what?" Lucie-Marie asked.

"I feel for certain that Daddy really likes that Cassie woman."

"There won't never be another woman right for Daddy 'sides our mama," Lucie-Marie said.

"I know that for a fact. Even if she won like Mama won at Madisonville. Won everythin' from pole-bendin' to bronc bustin'. I bet Cassie thinks she's almost as good as Mama, silly woman. Like somebody could just walk in here and take our mother's place or somethin'."

Annie Sharon strolled about the living room, nodding her head up and down as if she were trying to convince herself her younger sister was right. "That could never happen. Daddy loved Mama too much. 'Sides, we're doin' fine, just the three of us."

"But still I wonder if Daddy gets butterflies in his stomach, if his hands start sweatin', and he gets a lump in his throat when he's up close to that Cassie woman like I do with Diamondback." Annie Sharon cast a glance at her sister. "I don't know. Maybe it's thinkin' about the Silver Spur's special night for young folks that makes me feel like that."

"It can't be all Daddy's fault then. If being with Diamondback at the Silver Spur gets you to feelin' all growed up before your time, imagine what must happen to real grown-ups."

Annie Sharon said, "All I got to say is that Mama said our feelin's were nobody's business but our own."

I guess that means that Daddy's feelin's are his own business, too.

"I ain't sure."

"We could ask him," Lucie-Marie said.

Annie Sharon started getting annoyed with Lucie-Marie. "You know Daddy don't truck with no personal stuff, especially girl stuff. In a few years, I'll be a full-growed woman, and I know he don't want to think about that. If we come burnin' his ears with questions about love and huggin' and kissin', we'll be in plenty of trouble. I know that!"

"But, Annie Sharon, Mama would've talked to us about such things. Don't you think?"

"I don't know. She was awfully caught up with her animals, especially her stallion, Moncado. She spent hours and hours with him. He wouldn't let another soul ride him. Even now, Daddy is the only one who can touch him. He certainly won't let me ride him, though I know I'm ready. But will you stop with this 'Mama' stuff, please?"

Even though Annie Sharon did not want to talk about her mother, she too meandered toward the wall where Twanda's trophies hung on display. She fingered a belt, its bronc-busting buckle gleaming. She looked at it for a few minutes, sighed, and turned around to Lucie-Marie.

"Do you really think she rides with us, Lucie? I mean, when we want to win so bad we can taste it in the back of our mouths and our throats go dry? Is Mama watchin' over us when it's our turn at the gate?"

"I thought you didn't wanna talk about Mama."

"I don't. I just asked a question, is all. Can't I just ask a question?"

With a cowgirl hat perched atop her head and still wearing championship buckles and belts, Lucie-Marie stared at herself in a mirror that hung above a living room table. She took her own time about answering. "Well, for your information, Mama's always with me, horse or no horse, 'cause that's what mamas do. They tend their own. They love their own, whether you think she was there for us or not."

"Lucie-Marie, you don't even know what you're talkin' about. You can't remember her, but you're probably right. She's ridin' with you. If anybody knows, I know. But I'll tell you this. My memories of her don't do me one bit of good right now."

With that said, Annie Sharon walked away from the belts she had been studying and plopped onto the faded brown sofa across the room. "What kinda mother should I expect a dead woman to be? I shouldn't hold my breath waitin' for her tender touch. I know that."

Lucie-Marie did not answer. She spied one of her mother's spurs on the mantel. She attached it around her boot the same way as black troops who fought the Indians a long time ago. She grabbed her rope, twirled it in the air, and went romping around the room like a roper after a calf. "I don't know about you, but I know Mama rides with me."

The girls were so involved in their own fantasies, they did not notice Tie-Down enter the room. Shaking his head at Lucie-Marie's mess, he bellowed, "What in the world is goin' on in here? Annie Sharon, can't you control

Lucie-Marie any better that this? You know I told you two never to touch your mama's things. That's blaspheming the dead. Your mama worked too hard to win these belts and all this other stuff. Don't you go dressin' up and makin' fun with it, Lucie-Marie."

Tie-Down walked across the room to undo the tangle of belts and trophies Lucie-Marie wore. He carefully allowed the leather and silver to settle into a pile on the floor.

Tears welled in Lucie-Marie's eyes. "But, Daddy, we didn't mean no harm. We just wanted to feel like she was here with us. You know what I mean? We miss her, and this is as close to her as we can get, 'cause you won't say a thing about her or what she was like with us."

Tie-Down ran his fingers through his coarse brown hair. His chin dropped to rest on his chest. "It's bad enough I gotta raise you girls by myself. Now you want me to dig up memories of your mama as well. How much more you gonna ask of me? Sometimes I miss her so much I can't hardly stand it. I guess I know how you're feelin', but we gotta let go of her sometime, you know? She's been gone for years. We gotta accept the fact that it's just the three of us." His eyes narrowed as he stared out through a window into the shadows of early evening.

The girls quieted for a moment, afraid they'd pushed their daddy too far. It wasn't good if he got too sad. He would just get mad again because they were witnesses to his sadness. They knew Tie-Down liked everything to go smoothly and calmly—not the way things were headed this evening.

After a long, uncomfortable silence, Tie-Down shook a tan finger at his daughters. "Put your mama's things back where they belong," he said through clenched teeth.

"But, Daddy, I didn't do anythin'," Annie Sharon pleaded. "Lucie-Marie made all of this mess."

"But you're the oldest. You're responsible for her behavior." His shoulders drooped as his anger seemed to drain out of him. He changed the subject. "I see you fed and brushed down your horses. That's good. I didn't have to come after you for that. Got to tend to your animals every mornin' and every night, you know. You owe them that."

"I checked the calves, too, Daddy," Lucie-Marie said. "All eight of the new ones are accounted for."

"But, Daddy, she didn't tell you she got up close to Moncado. He almost kicked the livin' daylights outta her." Annie Sharon could not resist telling on her sister, who had brought up more recollections of their mother than she could handle. She'd fix her, all right.

"Good Lord, Lucie-Marie, how many times do I have to warn you to leave your mama's horse alone?"

"How can he still be Mama's horse if she's not here anymore? She's dead, Daddy. Somebody's gotta look after him, and ride him, and race him."

"Right now that somebody is me, and me alone. Moncado is a dangerous critter if he don't know you, if he don't know you're not afraid of him." Tie-Down paced across the room and back again. "Too much spirit, that's his problem. I always tol' Twanda that. Too much spirit for a quarter horse. Maybe she loved him so much 'cause they were just alike. Two of a kind, with too much spirit for this world."

Tie-Down sat in the rocker by the fireplace. Angry no more, he understood his girls were looking for something he could no more give them than he could make a peach cobbler or dandelion wine. Whatever was he to do with his young fillies, who had no mother to guide them and a father too rough and tumbling to do much more than say harsh words or stumble about the ranch in silence? And today of all days was not a time for the girls to get out of hand. This was all too much.

Tie-Down remembered Twanda on that out-of-control animal with his bucking, and neighing, and snorting. He remembered Moncado doing his best to get Twanda off his back, until he finally did. And he stomped her until she was almost unrecognizable. As Tie-Down recalled the horror, he shut his eyes tight. He struggled to stop his body from shaking. He knew shouting at his daughters would never stop the pain he felt when he thought about Twanda's death. The girls were children without a mother. He must find a way to help them live without her. But after all these years, he had failed to find a way to live without Twanda, himself.

Lucie-Marie stood and reached to the mantel to put a roping trophy back. Her fingers barely reached the shelf. So Tie-Down took the trophy from her hands and placed it for her. Lucie-Marie did not look at him. Her eyes studied the floor.

Annie Sharon made no effort to help at all. She sat on the edge of the sofa, staring into space.

"What's the matter with you? Didn't you hear me say to put these things away?" Tie-Down asked. His hands still shook as he tried to keep his pain and anger in control.

"Yeah, I heard you, Daddy," Annie Sharon answered.

"Then what do you call yourself doin'? You're sittin' there like a lump on a log."

"I wanna know somethin'."

"You want to know somethin'? You want to know? Well, gal, I gotta surprise for you. I want to know why you ain't mindin' what I say to you?"

"Daddy, I can't." Annie Sharon's arms pulled her knees against her chest.

"What you mean, you can't? It's pretty simple. Clean up these trophies!"

"That's not what I mean."

"Well, real quick, before I get a notion to whip your behind, what do you mean?"

"I want to know why you get so angry every time we mention Mama?"

Lucie-Marie said, "Annie Sharon, that's the question I keep askin' you. You get mad, too." Her words were little more than a whisper.

Tie-Down relaxed his tense shoulders. He let out a long sigh. "I don't get mad. I get bothered and frustrated with you bringin' up your mama's dyin' all the time; that's all. We're gettin' along all right."

"No, we ain't all right. I just wanna know more 'bout Mama. It's only natural. And I got a right to know. I'm her girl. Lucie keeps asking me stuff, and I don't have any answers. I was young myself when she died."

"Yeah, Daddy, we're her girls," Lucie-Marie added.

Tie-Down reached down to pick up a fine leather belt from the floor. Holding it clutched in his hands, he dropped himself onto the sofa with a thud. His eyes moved from one of his daughters to the other as he pondered how Twanda would have handled these questions if she were the one left behind. Oh, how the girls resembled their mother, and she loved them more than anything. She did. Nothing came before her girls. But how could he convince them she loved them more than life itself when she did, in fact, risk her life at the drop of a hat.

The smell of a wager sent her running for her gear. She would take anyone up on a bet; astride that fine horse of hers she could out-ride anybody, man or woman. But his girls were too young back then to remember that about Twanda. They remembered her not being with them for their first events. They probably knew she was seldom there for their bedtimes. They probably could not remember the ritual of her brushing and braiding their hair, that is, when she was not braiding Moncado's mane. The girls missed their mother, and he did not know what to do. Tie-Down did not know what to do with two eager, sad girls clamoring for their mother on the anniversary of her death.

"Okay, okay. You two come over here to your daddy, and I'll tell you somethin' about Twanda. Once we were comin' back from a rodeo near Tulsa. That's a long way, you know. I drove the truck with the calves and a few heads of cattle. Your mama was right behind me with Moncado and Macho, the horse I rode back then. She was followin' me home, you see. Well, like I said, the ride was a long one, and we were both tired after a whole day of competin'. Now we didn't do too badly that day, either. Altogether, we'd won a purse of a few hundred dollars and left some Oklahoma cowboys and girls red-faced, if I do say so myself.

"Anyway, as I was sayin', we were just goin' along. I must have fallen asleep 'cause I looked up to find myself sittin' in the middle of a cornfield, truck and all. And your mama? So trustin' she was. Well, she'd pulled right up 'long side of me. Like I must know where I was goin'. We were both exhausted, I guess. Too tired to get upset about the situation. So your mama just came over to the truck. Jumped right in beside me and fell asleep in my arms."

"That's so romantic, Daddy." Lucie-Marie moved closer to cling to his arm.

"Were the animals all right, Daddy?" Annie Sharon asked.

"Oh, everythin' was just fine."

"Well, tell us some more," Lucie-Marie begged.

"Daddy's said enough, Lucie-Marie. You're gonna tire him out." Annie Sharon narrowed her eyes at her sister. Tie-Down rarely gave this much. No need to push it.

"No. No, it's all right, Annie Sharon. I'd rather talk to you two about your mama than have you mopin' over her belts and trophies. That's not all there was to your mama. You've got to know that."

"Tell us another story, okay?" Lucie-Marie ignored her sister's warning.

"Well, let me see. Sometimes in the summer on an evening like this one, the sun would get to settin', all red and orange. Our magnolia and cypress trees seemed to reach up to the clouds that hung from the sky like cotton candy. With the grass smellin' ripelike, Twanda and me would jump on Moncado, that horse she set so much store by. We'd climb up on Moncado and walk him through the woods, past the corral. Walk him real slow so we could hear every sound that nature makes, everythin'. And then all of a sudden she'd kick Moncado up, and off we'd go, duckin' branches and jumpin' fences. I'll never forget fearin' Moncado fallin'. Me fallin'. Twanda would lean here and there, over thisaway and over thataway, barely missin' big ol' tree limbs. We crossed the brook and here comes water up my pants legs. Sometimes, I couldn't tell if your mama was on the horse, under the horse, or down in the brook drownin' to death. That woman didn't always use common sense when she was having fun. She would sing and nudge that animal into doing anything she wanted him to do. We could've been fallin' to the center of the earth. She wouldn't have cared. Humph!

"But yes, your mama was quite a horsewoman. I wish you could remember her better. Her cheekbones sat way up on her face like a Cherokee, real high and glowin'. Both of y'all look just like her. You do. Sometimes I see more of her than at other times, but always on this day. This is a hard day for your daddy. You gotta forgive me for not realizin' what a hard day this must be for the two of you, as well."

"Oh, Daddy, we just don't want you to be sad or think we don't appreciate how much you love us. Ain't that right, Lucie-Marie?"

"Well, I want to know what features I got that Mama had." Lucie-Marie ignored Annie Sharon's attempts to soothe Tie-Down. "How do I favor Mama?"

"Right there by your eyes, I imagine, Lucie-Marie. See how they arch up just so, like you always got a question on your mind?"

"I always knew I looked like Mama. I can tell from the pictures of her."

"What about me, Daddy?" Annie Sharon leaned toward her father.

"Your mouth."

"My mouth?" Annie Sharon puckered her lips, smiled with them, pursed them.

"Yes, your beautiful, full mouth. Your whole smile, when you get right down to it."

Tie-Down stared at his daughters, wondering if he'd done the right thing. Usually he didn't allow them to linger so long on thoughts of their mother. He believed it would make life even harder for them if they experienced the terrible loss he felt without Twanda in his life. "Well, you two are Daddy's rough, tough ridin' cutie-pies, that's for sure. And I love you way down deep in my soul."

Annie Sharon thought for a minute. "Daddy, was she smart, too?"

"Smart as a whip. I swear. Just like the two of you."

"You know Mama had to be smarter than you are, Annie Sharon." Lucie-Marie wrinkled her nose.

"All right, girls." Tie-Down shook his head. "That's enough of that. If I thought talkin' about your Mama was gonna cause you to fight, I would've kept my mouth shut."

"No. No, Daddy, don't stop."

Tie-Down caught a glimpse of night edging in through the curtains and determined this as an excellent time for the girls to go to bed. "Why don't you two get ready for sleep now? We got a huge day tomorrow. The Southwestern Rodeo Association's All-Star Rodeo over at the Diamond-L is gonna require all of our energy."

"We didn't forget that, Daddy. Did we, Annie Sharon?" Lucie-Marie beamed.

"Of course not. We're ready to stomp down, Daddy. I'm gettin' a good night's sleep, so I can race those barrels and bring home the gold," Annie Sharon boasted.

"Okay. It might be a good night to say your prayers. We're gettin' up as soon as the cock crows." Tie-Down kissed his girls on their foreheads before he went out to help Dupree Bonville, his foreman, lock the ranch down for the night.

Lucie-Marie thought of one more question. "Daddy, is Cassie coming with us?" she yelled after Tie-Down.

"Yeah, she is," he shouted back. "That all right with you?"

"Oh sure. I guess."

"All right then, I'll see y'all in the mornin'."

As soon as the girls were inside their room with the door shut, Annie Sharon grabbed her sister's shoulder. "Why does that woman have to go everywhere with us? Who does she think she is?" Annie Sharon fumed, breathing loud as she paced around the room.

"Well, maybe it's not so bad. I kinda like her. She's teachin' me how to tie knots, and make plant holders, and things."

"Some cowgirl you are. *'She's teachin' me to tie knots.'*" Annie Sharon mimicked her sister. "You ain't worth the time of day, talkin' like that. Well, she'll have to reckon with me if she thinks she wants to just waltz in here and take up with my father."

"But Daddy may be a little lonely?" Lucie-Marie tried to soften her sister's attitude.

"Everythin' Daddy needs done, we do it. And that's all there is to that."

Lucie-Marie didn't have the courage or the energy to contradict her sister again. Minutes later, she and Annie Sharon fell into an uneasy sleep.

chapter 2

Cassie Caruthers was a slip of a woman, not much bigger than a minute, but strong and handsome in a cowgirl sort of way. Her features mirrored those of a Mescalero Apache. Rumors were that she was a direct descendant of one of Geronimo's daughters and a Black Horse soldier in the Tenth Cavalry of the famous Horse Soldiers. Something about Cassie brought Twanda to mind for Tie-Down. Maybe it was just the sinews and strength of her body and her smiling attitude, ready to take on anything. Tie-Down needed to talk to Cassie tonight about his girls, who seemed ready to ambush her at every turn.

With the ranch secure for the night, Tie-Down picked up the telephone and asked Cassie to come over. A few minutes later, she arrived. She stood around in the kitchen while Tie-Down questioned her.

"When's the last time you and the girls talked?"

"The other day when you and Dupree were out mendin' pasture fences, I brought them lunch."

"Did they eat it?"

"They just sorta pushed the food around on their plates, letting me know, once again, I'm not their mama."

"Oh." Tie-Down sighed as if the weight of the world rested on his shoulders. "I just don't know what to do. You know how much I care for you, Cassie, but the girls are settin' this up like I have to choose between you and them."

"Don't forget their mother. Twanda figures in this, too. They don't want to think that any-body can come between you and their mother."

"C'mon over here, and let me talk some sense to you. My girls are a little possessive; I admit that. But if we let them get to know you, be around you, they'll change their minds."

Cassie pulled a chair close to the kitchen table and pulled a deck of Tarot cards from her bag.

"Oh no. Not your magic again. You know I don't hold with witchcraft and magic." Tie-Down's brow wrinkled, and he jammed his hands deep into the pockets of his tight black jeans.

When Cassie set her mind on finding out what the cards revealed, she did not hear him, and this was one of those times. He wondered how he managed to pick women with so much independence and eccentricity. Twanda used to throw bones about and leave food for her ancestors before every major rodeo event. She claimed it helped her ride better. And now, Cassie put her trust in the Tarot cards.

"Don't let the girls see you do this. They'll swear you put a spell on me."

"I did."

"Oh, Cassie, don't say things like that. It makes my bones tremble."

"And tremble they should. You're a good

man, Tie-Down. And Twanda was my good friend. When that horse went crazy on her, I was out there with the rodeo clowns, tryin' to distract that animal before too much damage could be done. But that wasn't God's will." Cassie closed her hand over one of Tie-Down's. "That was a long time ago. I'm looking at the cards to see what the spirits have in store for us now. You and me, Tie-Down. The two of us."

"Never forget, Cassie. I come with a total package. It's the four of us we've always gotta think of. You, and me, and my girls." He watched her shuffle the cards.

"And Twanda's not ready to give you up, either, according to these cards here. But there's no animosity toward me. It seems like she's paying more attention to the girls so they know that whatever happens 'tween you and me, they'll always come first."

Tie-Down seemed impatient with Cassie's reading. He went to the refrigerator. "Here, have some strawberry lemonade. Maybe I'll understand you better with a bit more sweetness in you."

Tie-Down smiled at Cassie, and she smiled back. The girls were in bed. The two adults could finally share a private moment together. Time to talk and a chance to rid each other of the loneliness that comes from living without a partner and racing from hither to yon all year long. "We got a big day tomorrow," Tie-Down said. "Might as well have some quiet time now. We'll be exhausted and cranky tomorrow unless, of course, every soul in this house comes home with prizes, some championship money, and smiles on their faces."

"You just watch us and see if we don't bring back the money," Cassie said.

She slowly drew another card. "That's right, and we've got some surprises to deal with tomorrow, too. The cards don't lie. The girls are up to somethin'. See? It says so right here." She pulled another card. "Now, Mistah Tie-Down Brown, I'm almost ready to say we ought to be together on a regular basis. It's good to have someone to talk to, and to cook for, and to love. Bein' with you is good for me."

"I don't rightly see how bein 'round me could be anythin' but good," Tie-Down said.

"Tie-Down, stop funnin' with me. I was serious. But then, I forgot. It's clearly possible that you don't have a serious bone in your body."

"Is that so?"

"Yep. I think ridin' all them wild horses has gone to your head, and you've got your brain all wiggle-waggled so you can't think straight."

"Who you sayin' can't think straight?"

"You, that's who."

"Well, let's see whose head is more wiggle-waggled. Is it too late to go race some horses?"

"Yeah, it is too late. But wait a minute. There's somethin' I gotta say. I always liked you, even when Twanda was livin'. I just kept thinkin', 'Now one of these days, I want to marry me a man like that Tie-Down Brown.'"

"If you win this race I'm suggesting we run, that may not be impossible."

"Wait, Tie-Down. I feel strange sometimes about my bein' with you, and Twanda's passing away. Maybe I just don't know exactly what to do with myself or with you, ol' wild man."

Awakened by voices, Annie Sharon climbed out through the window of her bedroom. Without

making a sound and with a stubbornness rival-
ing that of a mule, Annie Sharon crept around
to the side of the house where she could look
through a window into the kitchen. She saw
Tie-Down and Cassie standing close to each
other. Their arms wound about each other as
Tie-Down's face moved down to Cassie's. When
her father kissed the woman Annie Sharon
wanted out of their house and out of their lives,
Annie Sharon thought she was going to be sick.
Hot tears, brought on by anger and feelings of
helplessness, spilled down her cheeks. She
walked back toward the open window, her
clenched fists aching as her nails dug into her
palms.

Meanwhile, Cassie and Tie-Down sat down
again and continued to talk. They found themselves in a delicate situation that they both
wanted to make work. But they were not quite
sure how to go about making a family. Cassie
heeded the counsel of the Tarot, while Tie-
Down relied on his wit and his instincts.

Cassie shuffled the cards without flipping
them like a regular deck of cards. Tie-Down
always found it amusing how carefully and

respectfully Cassie handled the Tarot. She drew the Two of Cups, which showed a man and a woman prepared to make a toast.

"Look here, Tie-Down, the Two of Cups. That means harmony and marriage. C'mon over and look. Doesn't literally mean 'marriage,' but it predicts that relationships will go smoothly."

The tall man kept a gruff attitude so Cassie would not think him too much in love. The next card showed the Three of Swords, with the swords piercing a blood red heart while storm clouds raged about.

"Uh-oh." Cassie gasped. "Not so good. We've got somebody running interference."

"What d'you mean, somebody running interference?" Tie-Down asked, now fully interested in Cassie's reading, despite himself.

"Well, that usually means sorrow, anguish, even tears."

"Oh, that's all I need—three women out of control around here."

"No, Tie-Down, don't rush to conclusions. It's just a suggestion that someone's unhappy. And I think we both know who those someones might be."

"Annie Sharon and Lucie-Marie."

"You got it."

"Let's see the third card, Cassie."

"I don't know, maybe we should stop while we're ahead."

"Heck, no. Let's go on with it. I don't put much store in this stuff anyway."

"All right." Cassie chose the third card and leaned back in her chair.

"What's this? What does that mean, Cassie?"

"That's Death." Her hands trembled the slightest bit.

"Well, shucks. Then, ain't nobody in this family ridin' a horse tomorrow, rodeo or no rodeo."

Regaining her composure, Cassie gave Tie-Down a small, calm-down sort of smile and beckoned him closer. "Death doesn't mean 'death' the way you and I understand it. We'll all be ridin' as planned, and with God on our side as well. Don't be nervous."

"All right. But maybe you ought to explain what this Death means."

"It usually means change. See those bodies the horse is trampling on? Those can be situations or feelings that are being killed off by coming events. Maybe an idea somebody's holdin' on to will fall by the wayside, or an impossible dream might suddenly give way to reality."

"Well, put those away for now. You're givin' me the willies. Go on now, pack them up. I'm gonna go check on the girls."

Tie-Down crept into the bedroom where the girls lay asleep. He looked at them lovingly, gave each of their foreheads a peck of a kiss, and carefully removed one of Twanda's prize belts from Lucie-Marie's hands. Something had to happen, he thought. Something must happen so his girls could let their mama rest in Heaven. So the girls could get on with their lives. So all of them could go on. As he walked to place the belt back in a trophy cabinet, Tie-Down quietly asked Twanda to guide him, to release him, so he could free his family from living in the past.

"Twanda, please help the girls, and me, too. Help us to remember you and let you go at the same time. I know this is confusin', but imagine how this must be for them. They loved you so much. They can't make room for anybody else. Please help us, Twanda." Tie-Down felt relieved as he left the belt in the living room.

Back in the kitchen, he knew he needed to talk to Cassie again, to complete the conversation started earlier. "Cassie, there's somethin' I've been meanin' to tell you. I like you. I like you a lot, and I want my girls to like you. But I think the ghost of Twanda is standin' between all of us. What happened with Twanda, couldn't nobody stop it. Not me, or you, or the pickup guys who rushed out to save her."

Cassie opened her mouth to say something, but Tie-Down raised his hand.

"Twanda wasn't the kinda gal that had a stinginess to her. I bet my life that if I was gonna take up with another woman, she'd want it to be you," Tie-Down said.

"That's not quite what the cards say, but the ghost I see could be projected by the girls instead of Twanda. I'm not sure, but don't you be lyin' to me, you hear? Don't be sayin' things you don't mean just 'cause I spend so much time with you. I honestly can't remember a time when you talked about Twanda without raisin' all get-out, or gettin' your jaws so tight I thought I'd have to call the vet to pry your mouth open," Cassie said.

Tie-Down took Cassie's hand and led her to the worn but comfortable couch in the living room that looked out over his land. Even in the dark, the land gave Tie-Down solace and strength. Cassie lit candles that brought added softness and a peacefulness to the room which exhibited Tie-Down's and Annie Sharon's trophies, as well as those of his late wife. Photos showed Tie-Down with the best rodeo riders west of the Mississippi and even some riders east of the Big Muddy.

Fred Whitfield, the best calf roper of them all, stood right alongside Tie-Down at the Houston Livestock and Rodeo. Tie-Down posed with Inky Burroughs, a direct descendant of the Ibos, and one of the most famous cowboys of all time at the Bug Rodeo in Alvin last year.

Cassie's eyes swept the trophy wall, and she knew that no matter where she was going with this family, rodeo would remain a part of their future. Rodeo was in their blood. Cassie examined the pictures and turned to look at Tie-Down, who seemed to be off somewhere in another world.

"What's on your mind, honey? C'mon back to me," Cassie whispered.

"Well, it's still the girls. You know they were talkin' to me this evenin' and tellin' me they gotta right to know more about Twanda. And I guess I've come to decide they're right. She's half of whatever they are. They're half of her and half of me. It's just that, you know, sometimes I get this feeling that I don't understand 'em. It's like I can't talk to them 'less I'm carrying my razor strap, or I'm sure I gotta hairbrush stickin' out of my back pocket in case I need to keep them in line."

"You know for a fact that ain't right," Cassie said. "You're wrong to feel you have to beat sense into a child, ever. God knows, beatin' children ain't never done nothin' but made them completely angry and unruly. Yes, those that are abused and scorned gonna be partners with the Devil himself. Watch now, and see if what I'm sayin' ain't the truth. You won't be raisin' a hand to those girls so long as I'm around."

In her bedroom, Annie Sharon dozed in and out of sleep. Awake for a moment, she asked the Lord to bless her sister and her father, and to take Cassie away before she stole the place of her mother. A bright flash of lightning zig-zagged across the sky, and Annie Sharon was certain God answered her.

In the living room, Cassie saw the lightning, too. She believed God spoke to her, as well, implying the storm clouds over her new life would quickly disappear. She snuggled under a warm afghan, content and in high spirits. "You know what'll make me even happier right this minute?" she asked.

"Nope." Tie-Down hoped Cassie did not want to talk about the Tarot again, or how he raised his girls. He was not in the mood for that. He was doing the best he could, the best he knew how in raising the girls. Cassie's ideas did not set well with him. Cassie's way would prove too easy. The girls would end up spoiled, not ready for life's sucker punches and trials. Now was the time to toughen them up. He did not need Cassie presenting some whole new method of child-rearing, with no discipline and no punishments. He remembered his father locking him in his room when the old man wanted to get *his* attention. No. Just an easy "I'm sorry" would not serve as a solution to any and all of his daughters' pranks. Tie-Down looked out over the dark land. He knew every inch of it, like he knew the faces of his daughters. One day the land would be theirs. One day the TDB Ranch would belong to the girls. It was necessary they know horses, and cattle, and discipline the way other girls knew piano, or ballet, or singing.

"Stop daydreaming and c'mon over here to me," Cassie teased.

"What for? I ain't goin' nowhere away from you. I'm gonna be right here. And if I do go away, I won't be gone for long."

"Unless there's a rodeo comin' up in—oh, let's say in Colorado, huh?"

"Then I'd just load all of y'all up in a truck, and off we'd go."

"Tie-Down, you can't keep draggin' these girls outta school every time you need some cowhands. They've got to stay in school if they're gonna learn anything and finish."

"Don't start, Cassie. I know what I'm doin'. Their futures are right here in this land."

"All right then, let's talk about the ranch, the girls, and the rodeo. I love me some rodeo talk."

"Well, talking to you about that ain't a hard task."

"You talk to me, then, about the rodeo. I love me some cowboys. Show me a special cowboy, and I'll cook. I'll make some of my very special peach cobbler."

"I'm up for your peach cobbler."

"And I was just joshin' you. It's time for bed, and I gotta be goin' home now. Big day tomorrow. Meet you here 'round five o'clock in the morning, all right?

Annie Sharon and Lucie-Marie were late getting up. Lucie-Marie tugged at her sister's arm, trying to get her out of bed. The girls needed to tend to the chickens and pigs, feed and brush down the horses, and help load up the trucks. They only had an hour to do it all. But Annie Sharon would not budge.

"I'm not goin' anywhere," she said.

"What're you talkin' about—you're not goin' anywhere? You never miss rodeo days. 'Sides, Daddy said you can pick any horse you want for calf-ropin'."

"I'm not goin' because Daddy's carryin' that Cassie woman with us. I'm not goin' anywhere as long as she's goin'. Now leave me alone!"

"I'm gonna tell Daddy. That's what I'm gonna do. I can't believe you're lettin' some lone female keep you from ridin' today. I know Mama wouldn't take kindly to you actin' like this."

Lucie-Marie stood over her sister, who lay curled under her covers. What would their father do? She should tell him, but she didn't want to get Annie Sharon in trouble. The best thing to do was leave her be, and let Daddy find her all by himself.

"Well, I'm goin' now, Annie Sharon. I'm not comin' back, either. You better get your backside up!"

"Leave me alone!" Annie Sharon shouted.

"All right, if you wanna be like that, I'm gonna tell Daddy."

"I ain't goin' with that woman."

"Daddy's not goin' to like this at all," Lucie-Marie repeated. "You know he likes Cassie. You're just being mean about her; that's what you're doin'. And I'm gonna tell."

"Do whatever you want." Annie Sharon felt she must protest in this small way. What else could she do? She asked herself: *How else can I convince my father that Cassie wants to move in and take our mother's place?* Twanda Rochelle Johnson-Brown was the best female rider of all time, and this Cassie woman didn't hold a candle to Twanda's talent. And now, it looked as if her father had fallen for Cassie. What other way did she have to protest? Sure, she'd miss all of her friends. She'd miss competing against the rest of the girls in her league, but it would be worth it if she could show her father how she felt.

While Annie Sharon lay convincing herself of her brilliant plan, she heard the footsteps of Tie-Down Brown, heavy and deliberate. The footsteps came closer and closer. One after another, the clunk, clunk of a working cowboy's boots came toward her bed. When the clunks stopped, Annie Sharon's body shivered as she listened to the silence. A rush of chill morning air swept across her body as Tie-Down snatched her covers off.

"What's this foolishness I hear? You're not goin' because Cassie's goin'? Girl, you better move right along now. Get yourself ready. Help Dupree get the calves aboard that truck. Pick a saddle and a bridle for your events. Right now."

Annie Sharon did not move.

Like a snake striking through the air, Tie-Down's belt lashed across Annie Sharon's bottom and across her back.

The girl yelled in pain and surprise. She could not remember when Tie-Down had last struck her.

"You pile out of this bed right now. There's more where that came from, if you don't mind what I say. You're gettin' too grown for your own good. Now get on with it." Annie Sharon squirmed on the bed, struggling to move beyond her father's reach. "I ain't goin' nowhere with that woman. And that's all there is to it."

"Don't you contradict me, young lady." Tie-

Down's voice hissed through clenched teeth, low and gravelly. He leaned over to smack Annie Sharon with his belt again, but she managed to get out of bed on the other side. Rather than chase her all morning, Tie-Down stood back on his heels and said in a quiet voice, "We're all leavin' here in an hour. You are leavin', too. If you want to show up at the rodeo in your nightgown, that's up to you." He turned around and walked out as deliberately as he came in.

Annie Sharon's ears burned. She knew she had pushed her father as far as she dared. Now a dark brown welt ached and burned on her back. More of the same awaited her if she did not disgrace the memory of her mother by going on an outing with her family and this Cassie woman. All right, she would go, she decided, but she did not have to like it.

Outside, Lucie-Marie and Cassie fed the chickens and played with the new sheep Tie-Down had bought at auction. They were ready to help feed the horses when Tie-Down joined them.

"Mornin', Cassie. I'd be obliged if you saw to breakfast; I need to talk to Lucie-Marie about somethin'."

"Okay, I don't see a problem with that. I'm off right now. Lucie-Marie, what d'ya say to some hotcakes and bacon?"

"I say, 'Yes, ma'am!'"

Cassie headed toward the kitchen, leaving Tie-Down alone with his daughter.

"Lucie-Marie," Tie-Down began, "you know how much I loved your mama and how much I think about her. Why, I can't help but think about her every time I look at you and your sister. . . . It's just that there comes a time when everybody's got to get on with their lives. Think about the future. With you two girls to take care of and the ranch to run, I've got my hands more than full. . . ."

"Daddy, are you tryin' to say you really like Cassie, and you want us to like her, too?"

Tie-Down's mouth opened and closed a few times. His eyebrows moved upward. "Yeah, I guess I'm sayin' somethin' like that."

"Well, we figured that out already, me and Annie Sharon. But there's a problem, you know."

"Yeah, I know. But what do you see as the problem?"

"Cassie can't be our mother. She can be Cassie, and that's all right. That's fine, I guess. But she's not our mama, and she'll never be as good as our mama was for us. That's all we've got to say about that."

"Maybe that's all *you've* got to say, but Annie Sharon, I don't know. She's creatin' a big problem."

"Oh, I know. She don't take to Cassie at all."

"That's what I mean. I won't have her disrespectin' any grown-up the way she does."

"Daddy, if you fell in love with Cassie, what would happen to us?"

"Why, nothin' would happen to you, sweetheart. There'd just be twice as much love for you then as there is now. And there'd be somebody to help you with those woman things that I can't seem to get the hang of. That's all."

"Well, that's not what Annie Sharon says."

"Lucie-Marie, don't pay no mind to Annie Sharon; she's still a child, no matter how growed up she thinks she is. I'll sit down with you two, and we'll talk about all of this."

• • •

After her father left her, Annie Sharon crept away to the bathroom to shower and to inspect the welt disfiguring her back. Her father seldom raised a belt to her; when she was younger, Twanda had issued out the discipline. But Twanda usually only raised her voice. Maybe her daddy didn't know the power of his own hand, she thought. That must be the problem. Otherwise, he'd never have done this to her. The cotton of her nightgown stuck to the welt, making it sting all the more. She sat in the bathroom for a long time, crying. Crying because she wanted her mother, crying because Tie-Down had struck her, and because this Cassie was ruining their lives.

Meanwhile, Cassie had lost no time in throwing together a passel of hotcakes. When she had made as many as she thought two girls and a grown man could eat, she rang the bell that announced hot food, and she yelled to Lucie-Marie and Tie-Down. She pondered the whereabouts of Annie Sharon. She was probably deciding what to wear. Aha! Cassie made her way to the bathroom, where a long, old-fashioned tub with claw feet took up most of the space. Annie Sharon sat at the vanity she had convinced Tie-Down to build because Twanda once had one like it. A smile softened Cassie's face until she caught a glimpse of Annie Sharon's back. A gasp escaped her lips.

"How'd that happen to you, Annie Sharon?" Cassie asked quietly.

"Oh, I don't know. Things happen. I'm all right now."

"Let me take a look at that. I'll help you, Annie Sharon. I can tell by lookin' how much it hurts."

"No, really, I'm fine. Please leave me alone."

Cassie ignored Annie Sharon's protests. She surveyed the damage done to the girl's body. Her soft fingers touched the swollen red skin.

"Ow, that hurts."

"I know it does. I'm a nurse, you know. Do you have any hydrogen peroxide? I'll need some, and I'll get aloe vera from the garden. You sit still. I'll be right back."

Annie Sharon did not want to sit still. She did not want Cassie's help, either, but she had trouble putting her shirt on. She sat wondering what Twanda might have done in a situation like this. Probably the same thing Cassie intended to do. Annie Sharon shook her head. She sat at the vanity, confused, her head in her hands. She knew her daddy deserved a happy life. After all, when she grew up, she hoped her friend Diamondback would be in her life, too. But, right now, she and Lucie-Marie did not need another mother. That was the fact of the matter. When Cassie returned with the peroxide and the aloe, Annie Sharon managed to arrange her face into a scowl again. "This don't mean I'm dependin' on you for nothin', you know? I could've taken care of myself."

"Of course you can, Annie; nobody doubts that. I know you're a big girl. It's just that during the course of a day, this is what I do. Though I must say I learned this particular bit of medicine from my people, the Mescalero Apache."

"What do you mean, 'your people'? You're not Indian. You're darker than I am." A snort escaped Annie Sharon's throat.

"Well, that may seem true, just lookin' at me, but I'm one-quarter Apache. We'll have to go to a Pow-Wow one day. Your father tells me you're part Cherokee on your mother's side." Cassie dabbed the medicines on Annie Sharon's back and hips.

"Ouch! Daddy talks too much. And you don't know nothin' about my mother."

"Does he do this to you often, Annie?"

After a long silence, Annie Sharon said, "I don't have to talk to you about anything. Now go away, and leave me alone."

"If that's what you want."

"You heard me. Leave me alone, and take your redskin cures with you."

"There's no need to insult me, Annie Sharon. I wanted to help you."

"Well, I don't need no more help." Annie Sharon stood up. She winced as she struggled into her bra. She eased her long-sleeved riding shirt on, remaining stone-faced to hide her discomfort.

Cassie stepped away from her. "Annie, any time you want to talk, I'm here. And, by the way, breakfast is ready." Cassie walked back to the kitchen with heavy, dragging footsteps. What had she gotten herself into? Children in desperate need of a mother, but not willing to accept one. A father who took his frustrations out on the daughters he loved more than anything in the world, and a family that only came together in joy when they competed at a rodeo. Whatever was she to do? How could she get the girls to trust her? How could she get Tie-Down to hold his anger in and let his gentle side out?

Cassie heard Tie-Down and Lucie-Marie talking in the kitchen, so she hurried along. They had helped themselves to the hotcakes and bacon. "Be sure you leave some for Annie Sharon and me," Cassie said.

Tie-Down laughed. "If you come late for a spread like this, you're just outta luck. Right, Lucie-Marie?"

With a full mouth, Lucie-Marie nodded her head, her eyes smiling.

"Where's Annie Sharon?" Tie-Down asked.

"Oh, she'll be here directly," Cassie answered. She sat down and chewed on a strip of bacon. She stared at Tie-Down as he ate, shaken by what she had seen. There was no call to strap his daughter like that. No matter what happened, he could never justify raising his hand to his child.

In her room, Annie Sharon stood in front of
the mirror, almost ready to go now. She tucked
her regulation shirt into her tightest-fitting
jeans. She tugged her favorite boots on, and
pulled her bangs down so they showed under
her hat. Now, all she had to do was beat her
pal, Rosie Morales, in pole-bending and barrel-
racing. Tie-Down allowed her to calf-rope only
for exhibition, not in competition. Said it wasn't
ladylike. As if her mother appeared ladylike
when she was bronc riding. Well, he'd get
around to her way of thinking. But she must
stay on his good side, and apparently that
included her not being mean to Cassie or
embarrassing him in front of Cassie. Her
father's voice interrupted her thoughts.

"Annie Sharon," he called, "you're missin' a
great breakfast. You know better than to try
ridin' on an empty stomach. Get on out here
and join us."

"I'm not hungry, Daddy. I'll be okay. I'm goin'
out to check Tallulah. She's not in the truck
yet, is she?"

"Naw, I saved your animal for you to take
care of."

"All right then. I'm headed to the stables."

"Well, you're really missin' out on some rib-ticklin' hotcakes."

"Daddy," Lucie-Marie said in her sweetest, little-girl voice, "Daddy, when am I gonna get a horse of my own like Annie Sharon has? I'm old enough for lots of events, but I've got no horse."

"You want to try mine today, Lucie-Marie? Liberty takes to new riders real well."

"You mean it, Cassie? I could ride Liberty this afternoon?"

"Of course I mean it."

"Lucie-Marie, don't take advantage of Cassie. We've got plenty of horses for you to choose from," Tie-Down interrupted.

"But, Daddy, I want a horse that's used to a girl."

"Can't get used to a girl unless a girl rides it, to my way of thinking. Maybe that young mare we got would be a good choice."

"You mean Moncado's foal?" Lucie-Marie asked. "That's Mama's baby, isn't it?"

"Well, not actually. It's your mama's stallion's baby, only she ain't a baby no more."

"Oh, Daddy, I love you so much! I'd love to have her as my new horse. But I haven't spent much time with her. I think I'll ride Cassie's mare today, since Liberty's used to ridin' around the arena in exhibition and racing barrels."

"Lucie-Marie, I didn't say the horse was yours. I said you could ride her." But Tie-Down's words floated in the air right over Lucie-Marie's head as she ran off to find a saddle she could use on Liberty.

Tie-Down and Cassie were left alone. Cassie thought this might be a good time to bring up the subject of the welts on Annie Sharon's back.

"Tie-Down, I spent some time with Annie Sharon this mornin'."

"Good. I tol' you it would just take a little time for them to warm up to you."

Cassie wondered how he could act as if nothing happened this morning. "She has welts on her back."

"She's gotta learn to mind me."

"Tie-Down, these days, beating a minor is called child abuse."

"Oh, c'mon. That's how I was raised, and I'm not complainin'. Discipline is really important for children. They gotta learn respect for their elders. A little whippin' never hurt nobody."

"Well, if you want me to be a part of your life, that's got to stop. You can't raise your hand to these girls. I mean it."

"Well, in the last few months, Annie Sharon's been gettin' too big for her britches. She's got a really bad attitude. How do you propose I get the girls to do what they have to do?"

"Just talk to them, that's all. It may take longer, but that's how you really reach them."

"Aw, I shoulda known an educated gal like you would misunderstand how I raise my girls. And if I didn't care so much about you, I'd tell you to mind your own business. But I'll do my best to 'talk' to them for your sake. But I'm not promisin' anythin', because they really get me upset sometimes."

"I suspect that sometimes you're upset because of somethin' else. But what you propose is a fair deal. Wanna shake on that?"

"Naw, I wanna hug on that."

Out in the barn, Annie Sharon brushed

Tallulah down, getting ready to braid her mane and tail with colorful ribbons. The excitement she felt about the rodeo allowed her to push the incident with her father to the back of her mind. She concentrated on Tallulah, a beautiful horse, sixteen hands tall and as strong as they come. Annie Sharon felt there was no way she could lose on the back of this wondrous black animal with tufts of white between her ears. She murmured into Tallulah's ear, explaining how the two of them would win first place racing barrels. The mare nuzzled her head against Annie Sharon's shoulder. Both Annie Sharon and the horse whirled around, startled, as Lucie-Marie raced into the barn, panting for breath.

"Where you runnin' to?" Annie Sharon asked.

"To get Liberty used to me. Cassie said I could ride her this afternoon in the exhibition for us young people."

"My, my, my. That's awfully nice of her. Do you think Daddy's lettin' her be so nice to us on account of the fact he likes her so much?"

"Who cares?"

"Well, I do. 'Cause, like I tol' you, I'm not gonna be suckered into lettin' some other woman take Mama's place."

"Well, I do think she's awfully nice."

"You would. I keep forgetting that you don't remember Mama as well as I do."

"Why do you keep holdin' that over my head like I don't have any feelings for Mama? Annie Sharon, that's not fair."

"I'm not thinkin' about fair. I'm thinkin' about loyalty."

"You ain't right, Annie Sharon. You've got a bad attitude just like Daddy says you do. Treating Cassie nice doesn't have to mean we ain't loyal to Mama."

Lucie-Marie took Liberty's tether and headed out to the corral. "I don't want to talk to you anymore, Annie Sharon. You just want to be difficult and trifling."

Annie Sharon watched her sister handle the frisky Appaloosa with a certain kind of pride. She did not expect Lucie-Marie to manage the horse so well.

Lucie-Marie rubbed her hand along the horse's shoulder and spoke to Liberty in a soothing voice. "Let's go on outside and get used to each other. Plus we wanna pick out a saddle. A real pretty one, 'cause we're gonna show off today." She yelled back over her shoulder to her sister, "Annie Sharon, I ain't payin' no real attention to you at all. Cassie's lettin' me ride her own horse. That's pretty friendly. That's all there is to it. Right, Liberty?"

Lucie-Marie jumped onto Liberty's bare back, holding on to her only by her mane. She tightened her thighs around the horse and dug her heels into her sides so Liberty would break into a run. Off they went, away from her sister's sour face, away from Cassie and her daddy, and into the field behind the house. Wildflowers, corn, collards, tomatoes, and okra lined the path she took. She knew no happiness that equaled what she felt when she rode bareback. No matter that it was how her mother got trampled. In Lucie-Marie's mind, her mother had challenged God, trying to take on a horse that was not fully broken.

But Liberty was a marvel. She galloped them past the vegetables and through a grove of trees where fog still hung low in the early light of morning. She followed each and every nudge of Lucie-Marie's body until they returned to the stables.

"Annie Sharon, this horse is incredible. Like ridin' the wind, I tell you. Gosh, I hope Cassie lets me ride her all the time."

"Don't count on it. Besides, isn't Daddy takin' you to an auction on your birthday so you can buy your own horse?"

"How am I gonna find a horse like Liberty?" Lucie-Marie sighed as she used a hose to shower the sweating Appaloosa with fresh, cool water.

"You won't. You have to train your own horse, and love her so she moves like a part of your body. Take time with her. Make her your own. That's how you get a horse like Tallulah or Liberty. No matter how good Liberty feels to you, your own horse'll feel better 'cause you'll know you can trust her."

"You think so, huh?"

"Yep."

"But you know? We're runnin' late," Lucie-Marie said. "We'd better go ahead and help Dupree get all of the calves and steers in the trucks. Best hurry, or Daddy'll be mad."

"I'm just waitin' on him, is all. It's his ranch, after all. Nothin' happens 'less Daddy says so."

"What's keepin' him?" Lucie-Marie wondered aloud. "Said he wanted to leave real early."

"Don't be so thick-headed. You know who's keepin' him."

"Annie Sharon, for goodness' sake, give them a break, will you?"

Annie Sharon threw a saddle on Tallulah. She fastened belts and buckles so she would be ready to herd the last of the animals when her father showed up. She hated this business of transporting the animals. But she knew owning all of the animals used at a rodeo proved a big moneymaker for her family. And what better way to know, firsthand, the personalities of each animal? Annie Sharon knew Madness, Last Draw, and Rodan as three of the roughest bulls on the rodeo circuit. Smooth Talker, White Water, and Delilah could be tricky critters, calm one minute and wild as all get-out the next.

The same proved true with the horses, but she had a way with all of them. They knew Annie Sharon's smell and her touch because she fed them and bathed them. Plus, the family made money every time someone tried to ride an animal in a competition. Each attempt put money in her father's pocket whether the rider won any money or not.

With Tallulah saddled, Annie Sharon changed her mind and trotted the horse up to the house. "Daddy, ain't it time to finish loading up yet?"

"Sure 'nough is, Annie Sharon; thanks for remindin' me. I got caught up talkin' with Cassie here."

"I bet," Annie Sharon mumbled under her breath as she rode off.

chapter 3

The trucks the Browns used to transport their animals had seen better days. Dents served as reminders that the bulls could be a bit too rambunctious. The worn chains that locked the animals in had wire added to hold them together. Threadbare tires needed replacing with new ones.

Annie Sharon stood ready to help the men herd the animals out of the corrals, through the chutes, and into the trucks. Though her father cautioned her often about the bulls and the wild horses, Annie Sharon was too sure of her skills as a cattle herder to pay him much attention. She and Tie-Down often butted heads. He believed in the old ways that had come down to them from generations of Texas cowhands. Learn first to herd on foot, they said, then take it up with horses.

But Annie Sharon began working with horses early. Ever since she had been able to walk, she exhibited a love of horses. As a toddler, she rode in the saddle with her daddy to the market, out to the grazing land, and all over the hundreds of acres the ranch spread itself across. Tie-Down said it was more important to hold on to the land than worry about whether or not the barn was painted, or whether the roof leaked sometimes. None of that interested Annie Sharon, but she loved the animals. She was a cowboy's cowgirl, and she intended to stay one all of her life.

With everyone pitching in, the trucks soon bulged with calves, steers, and horses. The family, Cassie, and several animals occupied one truck, while Dupree drove a second truck with the remainder of the animals.

Following the signs to Navasota took Brown and Company down several narrow twisting roads with little traffic. The trucks barreled through one small town and then the next. Though the ride was peaceful enough, Annie Sharon's heart remained heavy. Earlier, she had wanted to go to this rodeo, but now she did not care if they went or not.

Tie-Down and Cassie laughed and joked about the most ridiculous things, and Lucie-Marie enjoyed the conversation like this was a family outing.

Annie Sharon focused on the landscape flashing by outside the window. She refused to participate in the light banter that filled the truck. Today's rodeo schedule included one of the greatest black bull riders in the country. Earlier, Tie-Down had promised to introduce his girls to Hank Crawley himself. Usually when Annie Sharon came upon a perk like this, she reveled in how special her daddy treated her. But today she only saw how special he treated Cassie. It could not be fitting that adults teased, and giggled, and blushed so much. Why, even she and Diamondback never carried on like this.

But before she could work herself into a terrible fit, Annie Sharon heard the rumble of other trucks. She knew that meant they were close to the Diamond-L, where folks she had known all of her life were getting ready for a fine day of eating, dancing, riding, and roping.

"How much farther is it now?" Annie Sharon asked.

"Oh, just a little ways," her father said in a nonchalant way that made Annie Sharon feel he thought he talked to a child, not a girl almost grown.

Cassie added in her two cents as if somebody had asked her something. "Annie Sharon, there're some great little shops here with antiques and real cute clothes. We could check them out after we drop off the animals. If you want."

Lucie-Marie jumped in, "Oh yes. Let's go. I need an armoire. Isn't that what you call it, Daddy, an armoire? I need a mirror of my own."

Annie Sharon's head spun. She wanted to scream. She could not resist snapping, "What do ya wanna look at your ugly self for, Lucie-Marie?"

Lucie-Marie snapped back, "'Cause I'm

worth lookin' at, that's why. I don't always wear a scowl on my face like you do, you know?"

Cassie knew ruffled feathers needed smoothing. She said, "It was just a suggestion, girls. I didn't mean for you to jump down each other's throats."

Tie-Down became annoyed as well. "You two hush up. I've had about as much of your squabbling as I'm gonna take. You keep it up, and I'll turn this truck right around. You can spend the day in your room."

This outburst helped to convince Annie Sharon that Cassie was the reason for her father's sudden meanness to her. It used to be that she was his favorite. Now he was just as likely to snipe at her as to say something nice. It was all Cassie's fault.

"We're here!" Lucie-Marie shouted. Her eyes shone, and a smile spread across her face as she peered through the windows of the truck. She spied hordes of pickup trucks, horse trailers, and the wrought-iron fencing that read, DIAMOND-L.

Tie-Down drove through the gate and stopped to greet Sam Meeks, who directed him to park near the corrals constructed to contain the livestock.

The expression on Annie Sharon's face changed now. She wanted to see her friends Diamondback, Rosie M., Tookie, and Bubba. Bo-Beep should have arrived by now, too. The warm summer air seemed to crackle with excitement. Laughter and the hum of cheerful conversation filled the air outside the arena. The aroma of burning mesquite, barbecue, and roasting slabs of beef drifted throughout the grounds.

Tie-Down knew his daughters wanted to go looking for their friends. He also knew the work of unloading the trucks must be done first. "Soon as we get these animals situated, y'all can go socialize. But don't forget to come back to get ready for your events. I'm not gonna saddle your horses for you like I did last time. You caught me off guard, then, in a sweet mood. Today, I'm just sweet." The girls laughed. So did Cassie, who liked this easy, funny side of Tie-Down.

Tie-Down dropped the back gate of one truck after he opened the corral, and the steers and cattle thundered out. Dupree opened the second truck to release the horses. He led them to the back of the truck, where he tethered them to the corral fence. Only Moncado gave Dupree trouble. Annie Sharon suspected Moncado gave trouble because he had never learned to respect anyone but Twanda. It was still a mystery to everyone in the group as to why Tie-Down insisted on bringing Moncado to every rodeo. Annie Sharon thought it might be his way of honoring her mother. Lucie-Marie was of a mind Twanda sat right there on that horse, all the time, and that was why nobody else could mount him.

The girls waited patiently and watched the men get the animals into place. When the trucks stood empty, the two of them disappeared into the crowd.

"Well, at least we made it here without a real squabble, darlin'," Cassie said.

Tie-Down nodded. "So I see. This is a good time for the girls to get a real feel for you, Cassie, when they see you on Liberty, racing those barrels."

"Yes. And calf-ropin'," Cassie added. "I hope you heard me. I said, 'Yes, and calf-ropin'." Cassie covered her face with her hands and peeked through her fingers at him. "Maybe I'll even go for the bareback ridin' today. I'm feelin' mighty lucky." She smiled and chuckled. "If the spirits are with us, you might be ridin' home with three championship rodeo gals. Not just me, but Annie Sharon and Lucie-Marie, as well."

"Oh Lord, don't wish that on me. My truck won't hold all those swelled heads."

Cassie pretended to strike at him with her hand. But Tie-Down darted out of her reach, laughing.

The sun, high in the sky by this time, left the ground shimmering with heat. Annie Sharon thought it almost too hot to run a horse or do any trick riding. She ambled toward the grand-stand. In brilliant prairie light like this, she would surely see Diamondback's tall, thin fig-ure. Long-limbed, and sporting an air of arro-gance, Diamondback could certainly be found parading his horse somewhere near the arena.

Annie Sharon decided to go back to the corral

and saddle up Tallulah. It might be easier to find this young man she considered her boyfriend, if she rode around the area. But once she sat astride Tallulah, she did not have to look for Diamondback. She rode only a short distance before the seventeen-year-old found her.

Diamondback, or Arthur Littleton which was his real name, seemed to be a mixture of everyone who had passed through Texas in earlier days. He sported the high cheekbones of the Lakota Sioux, the silvery-gray eyes of the German settlers, and the square face of the Aztecs.

"Hey, where you on you way to?" Diamondback asked as he drew his horse, Lightning, close to Annie Sharon and Tallulah.

"Well, hey yourself, Diamondback," Annie Sharon said, hiding a grin. "I'm off to pay my fees so I can compete today."

"Yeah, I already paid mine. Almost wiped me out, too, but I saved a little so I could take you to a movie show."

"That was really nice of you, Diamondback, but you know my daddy. We'll have to promise to be back before the sun goes down."

"But, Annie, I wasn't gonna pick you up till the sun was down," Diamondback quipped. He laughed. "Never you mind; I'm just playin' with you, Annie."

"Well, after sundown's not gonna happen. We'll have to go in the afternoon when all the little kids are there. That's just how my daddy is," Annie said. "But I still wanna go."

"All right, then." Diamondback smiled at her. "We'll go. Come on, I'll ride you over to the office so we can talk for a while. What are you ridin' in?"

"I'll tell you if you promise not to say a word to a soul," Annie Sharon whispered. "I'm goin' to do bareback, barrels, and pole-bendin'!"

"That's quite a lineup. Does your daddy know?" Diamondback waited for her answer. "Uh-oh, he doesn't know, does he? Well, I'm not goin' to get in the middle of that. He don't take too well to me already."

"I know I can trust you, Diamondback. These days I can't talk to anybody."

"Why not? You and your pa were always so close." Diamondback stared at her, wondering what the problem might be.

"Just because. Things are a little different now, that's all," Annie Sharon murmured, speaking almost to herself. "Let's go find Mr. Stephens so I can pay up. Okay?"

"Sure," Diamondback said. He sat tall in his saddle, his smooth tan face glistening around a mole on his cheek that Annie Sharon considered cute.

She felt his dark, deep-set eyes riveted on her. He reminded her of her favorite rap star. When Diamondback stared at her like this, Annie Sharon blushed.

Diamondback found this attractive. His blushing gal, he thought. "Well, Mr. Stephens is 'round to the office. Let's go see him."

With that, Annie Sharon and Tallulah trotted ahead. It was never hard to spot Mr. Stephens. He possessed a wiry body like most cowboys, and his skin was roughened from the sun like most cowboys. But he had only one arm. That made him easy to find in the crowd of cowboys at the office; not many cowboys riding around with one arm and a cigar. Still, taking Mr. Stephens lightly would be a mistake. More than one cowboy had found that out the hard way. Mr. Stephens roped, and rode, and lassoed with the best of them.

The two young people made their way around the picnic tables full of families sharing barbecue, fried chicken, potato salad, and strawberry lemonade. Annie Sharon didn't see a soul she could not name. The Cook family with the girl triplets sat in this group. So did the Wagoners with the flat-headed boy, Scratch, who was always picking on Lucie-Marie. A little farther along, Annie Sharon caught sight of Rosie Morales, her best friend. Rosie M. sat at a table, her long, dark hair cascading to her waist. A Chicana with an impish face, Rosie M. crinkled her nose and smiled at her friends when she saw them.

"Hey, Rosie M., you ready for this afternoon?" Annie Sharon asked.

"You bet I am. I'm jus' finishin' up my lunch now. I already saw Mr. Stephens to pay him my fee for ridin'. The lineup's gettin' long. I know you must've already seen him, Diamondback. What's up, Annie Sharon?"

"We're on our way over there right now, Rosie M."

"All you've got to do is sniff for the smell of that cigar."

"We know that much is true," Annie Sharon said, giggling.

"Okay, you two know where I'll be. Warmin' up Bebo. We're runnin' off with all that money today. Why don't y'all jus' take a seat in the bleachers, 'cause Rosie M. here is gonna win everythin'!" Rosie M. laughed a little before she added, "I'm really not kiddin'. You better take me serious. I'm gonna give y'all a real run for your money today."

"We'll see about that," Annie Sharon said. She nodded a signal to Diamondback that they should be going. They waved a good-bye to Rosie M., and nudged their horses along.

The scent of food hung heavy on the air. So did the scent of manure and the animals that created it. Voices rang out as cowboys greeted old friends, and cowgirls yelled hello to women they had competed with at the last rodeo. At the office, a crush of riders almost threw money at Mr. Stephens and Big Al. Guys and women who usually worked in construction, as medical technicians, teachers, or grocers crowded around Big

Al. Today was their day to be cowboys and cow-girls.

Annie Sharon felt pride that she came from a family that took rodeo seriously, not like a Saturday morning hobby or a dream from childhood. But she understood the joy the "once a week" participants must be feeling. To Annie Sharon, in the whole world nothing compared to the power of having a good horse galloping underneath her, as if God had suddenly given her wings. Yeah, she understood.

Mr. Stephens finally noticed Annie Sharon among the jumble of green, red, white, and plaid regulation shirts, the ten-gallon hats, and the leather chaps. "Hey, ain't you Twanda's oldest?" he asked.

"Why, yes, sir, Mr. Stephens. And you're just the man I been lookin' for. You got space for another barrel racer, pole-bender, and bare-back rider?"

Mr. Stephens stared at Annie Sharon with a smirk. "Got space for barrels and poles, but no bareback for you, 'less I talk with your pa first. How does that suit you?"

"Well, okay. Mr. Stephens, I'll do with the

barrels and poles this time, but next time I
want whatever events I got the money for."

"Well, missie, we'll see what your pa says.
But where's your money for the barrels and
poles? That's the issue now." He reached a cal-
lused hand across the counter. Annie Sharon
counted out sixty dollars, handed it to Mr.
Stephens, and asked again, "You sure about
the bareback, Mr. Stephens? I've got the
money."

"Yeah, and I got one arm. So how's that
change what I tol' you?"

"Okay, Mr. Stephens. Thanks." As she rode
off with Diamondback, Annie Sharon heard
Mr. Stephens retelling the story of her mother's
fatal attack in an arena, and how he was having no part in taking another of Tie-Down
Brown's girls to destiny's door.

"Sorry about that, Annie Sharon." Diamondback tried to console her. "Maybe next time
he'll just take your money just like anybody
else's."

"Oh, I'm all right, Diamondback. I just wish
folks would stop treatin' me like I got a curse
on me or somethin'." Annie Sharon lifted her

hat, shook out her bangs, and donned the hat again. Diamondback did not see the tears in the inside corners of her eyes.

"You know how superstitious cowboys can be, Annie. They don't mean no harm," Diamondback said.

Annie Sharon shook her head, trying to clear the vision of her mother being trampled by her wild horse. Instead, she thought about Bill Pickett, a cowboy of long ago, who had invented bull wrestling by watching how dogs worked cattle. She heard Pickett started by grabbing bulls by their horns and twisting their necks until they rolled over. Her mind wandered to Mary Fields, who was as big as any man and who could shoot, fight, or lasso anything put in front of her. Annie Sharon remembered stories of the Tenth Cavalry, the Horse Soldiers, all black except for the officers, who were sent to make the West safe for settlers against the Indians. On horseback, the Cavalry was a powerful force.

Annie Sharon looked down at the one spur she wore because the Horse Soldiers only wore one spur on their boots. But it seemed that because of her mother's death, some people wanted to stop her from living out her dreams; people who would prevent her from mastering the skills an all-around cowgirl should have.

Annie Sharon meant no disrespect to her mother, but she knew of hundreds of cowboys and cowgirls who had lived earlier and left her rightful legacies as well. As she and Diamondback rode along, the fourteen-year-old thought about the all-black towns, like Tulsa's "Little Africa." She felt some folks just did not understand the wave of history she planned to ride upon, with their help or without it.

With a couple of hours left before the rodeo actually began, Annie Sharon had time to warm Tallulah up. She felt a need to be by herself, to figure out the different feelings she experienced. She must not go into the arena with a confused mind. Focus would be absolutely necessary.

"Diamondback, I need a bit of time alone with Tallulah now. Do you mind?"

"No, I don't mind at all. Whatever you say, Annie." Diamondback galloped off in the direction of some of his friends who raced their horses on the open prairie.

Annie Sharon thought all of her feelings rested like a big lump in the middle of her chest. She told herself she would not wallow in sadness. Today was a special day, and she would win some prizes. She thought for a minute she wanted to cry, but that was not the problem, either. She sat on Tallulah without moving a muscle for a time. Then she rubbed a hand along the warm hair of the mare's shoulder and closed her eyes for a moment.

She needed a break from Twanda. That was what pulled at her. Everybody saw "Twanda's oldest." Nobody saw her, Annie Sharon. They looked at her and saw a ghost instead of a young girl with red blood running through her veins and dreams that were possible if she willed herself to be disciplined and daring. That was the problem. That was the weight resting heavy on Annie Sharon's shoulders. And on her soul.

How was she going to get around the fact of everybody feeling sorry for her? Pampering her? So today she would not bronc-bust. Maybe next time she would go ahead and speak to her daddy. Maybe next time with some planning, she would get her way. She heard once that the best thing to do with somebody standing in your way is to get him on your side. Annie Sharon knew Mr. Stephens trained lots of girls to calf-rope and to ride bareback. She would become one of them. Then it would be in his best interest to show her off as championship material. She would get to ride.

With her problem all solved, Annie Sharon went looking for Rosie M. and Lucie-Marie.

Lucie-Marie had gone off in search of her friend Bo-Beep. Bo-Beep, a masterful cowhand, enjoyed other interests, too. For instance, Bo-Beep knew the names and features of virtually every kind of Texas wildflower, and he was an excellent trick roper. Bo-Beep usually entertained the crowd between rodeo events with huge rope loops around his body, flat loops between his legs, reverse loops, and rollovers. He also performed tricks called the rolling butterfly and the ocean wave.

These roping tricks fascinated Lucie-Marie almost as much as the flower garden she now found herself standing in. Mama Big Al, as Big Al's wife was called, kept acres of nothing but wildflowers and trails for exploring them. Lucie-Marie was not surprised to find Bo-Beep among the rare and beautiful colors. Mama Big Al sold some of her flowers to wholesalers in town, who sold them to folks too civilized to grow wildflowers in their own gardens. Mama Big Al wore jewelry and bright colors just like the ones in her garden, especially on rodeo days.

Mama Big Al liked to hang out with Bo-Beep because he appreciated her careful grooming of the scarlet and yellow Mexican hats, the lavender fluff of mealy sage, the amber and cream meadow rue, and the startling white of jimsonweed. Of course she nurtured the bluebells and the Indian paintbrush, but those two grew in spite of care, not because of it.

When Lucie-Marie found her two unlikely friends, she basked in the scent of the flowers and the flurry of chatter between Bo-Beep and Mama Big Al, who always had a story to tell about one cowboy or another. Plus, Bo-Beep was continually trying to convince Mama Big Al of the reality of his armadillo races; they were not just a figment of his imagination, he insisted.

Mama Big Al chortled. "Bo-Beep," she said, "those armadillos don't know they're in no race. They don't even go in straight lines."

Bo-Beep replied religiously every time, "Every race don't have to go in a straight line; you got to use your imagination like I do, Mama Big Al."

Without batting an eye, Mama Big Al said, "If I used my imagination like you do, Bo-Beep, they'd carry me away from here in a straitjacket. Now I don't mean no offense to your imagination, Bo-Beep, but there'll be no illegal armadillo racing on the Diamond-L. If you should plan on goin' against my wishes, then there's always Big Al himself to answer to. You understand?"

Bo-Beep nodded his head, and they both laughed. Then he talked to Lucie-Marie about the various blossoms she stood among that almost hid her face. When the discussion of flowers ended, Lucie-Marie asked Bo-Beep if he knew any girl trick ropers.

Bo-Beep always thought for a while when she asked him this question. He said, "No, can't rightly say I do, but that don't mean there ain't any. Just means I ain't heard of 'em."

Lucie-Marie did not carry the conversation much further, but she asked Bo-Beep to make her a honda, or a knot for a beginner's rope, so she could learn some spinning tricks to show her father. Since Annie Sharon had no interest in spinning tricks, Lucie-Marie felt this could be something she did on her own, the first in her family. Bo-Beep cautioned that rope spinning should be learned slowly, but Lucie-Marie, in her excitement, held the honda too tightly, and the rope kinked up right on top of her body.

"See? I tol' you, Lucie-Marie. You gotta go slow." Bo-Beep demonstrated a flat loop by standing with his feet apart, his long body bent slightly forward at the waist. His arms held the loop in his hands about eighteen inches from the honda. Then his left hand turned the rope loose, and he threw the loop away from his body to let a twirl begin.

"Oh, Bo-Beep, I'll never get that," Lucie-Marie whined.

"You sho' enough won't, if you keep sayin' so." Bo-Beep handed the rope back to her and checked his watch. "We should be makin' our way to the arena right about now." Lucie-Marie hitched her spinning rope to her jeans and pranced along beside Bo-Beep, one of the most reliable rodeo pickup men anywhere in Texas. He even worked the Houston Livestock and Rodeo Show. Fort Worth's, too. Lucie-Marie admired Bo-Beep as a cowboy who went to the aid of any competitor in danger in the arena. When bulls got out of control or a bronc tried to stomp a cowboy, Bo-Beep and the rest of the pickup men raced to the rescue.

Lucie-Marie wanted to ride pickup one day. Trophies looked less and less important to her. Now that she had spent time with Bo-Beep, she realized if somebody really quick and strong like Bo-Beep had been working the day Moncado stomped her mother, Twanda might actually still be alive. Yeah. Talking to Bo-Beep was truly revealing.

Lucie-Marie felt good. She wore regulation rodeo getup: a long-sleeved shirt and a hat so she could participate in the gala entry of the riders. Plus, she was going to enter on Liberty, Cassie's horse. She would appear impressive to anyone who took the time to look at her. And of course she would be noticed riding next to Bo-Beep in his black and silver on his mulberry Andalusian. The dappled, purplish-gray of the animal brought out the purple in Bo-Beep's beautiful blue-black skin. Yeah, Lucie-Marie Johnson-Brown had found herself a new riding partner for sure. And maybe in God's eyes, it was better to be about the business of saving competitors' lives than winning money.

"Lucie-Marie, ain't you gotta horse of your own yet?"

"No, sir, Bo-Beep. Not as yet. Today I'm ridin' Cassie's Liberty."

"Well, you're goin' to have to do somethin' about that, 'cause in order to be a premiere trick roper, you gotta be ridin' at the same time you got your spinnin' goin'."

"I know, Bo-Beep."

"Lucie, take my word for it—I've seen some Mexican vaqueros do rope tricks standin' in their saddles. Takes your breath away, it does."

"Wow, Bo-Beep, you think I could ever be that good?"

"All it takes is practice, sweetheart. Concentration

and practice, and a little trust that your rope and your horse will work with you, and not against you." The two friends quieted, deep in their own thoughts as they walked toward the arena.

The U.S. and Texas flags billowed in the wind as Mr. Stephens and Big Al held them at the front of the parade. Black and Mexican cowboys and girls sat on their horses, ready to gallop in a big circle around the whole of the arena. Lucie-Marie spied Cassie atop Liberty and could not believe her eyes. Why would Cassie ride Liberty after promising the horse to her? Lucie-Marie felt her hopes dashed. She could not ride in the grand opening without a horse. Twelve was too old to ride with Tie-Down or Bo-Beep; that was for little girls.

Annie Sharon caught sight of her sister, who looked so bewildered and disappointed that Annie Sharon felt she must do something. The two of them had talked and planned this day for a long time.

Annie Sharon rode Tallulah over to her sister, grabbed Lucie-Marie up, and let her sit behind her on the saddle. But instead of taking their place in line, Annie Sharon rode Tallulah back toward the truck where Moncado stood tied to a corral fence.

"You goin' to ride Mama's horse? Ain't nobody rode Mama's horse, except for Daddy. Even Dupree don't try to ride him," Lucie-Marie said. Her eyes darted from Annie Sharon to the horse and back again.

"I'll be all right, Lucie-Marie. I remember somethin' Mama tol' me. She said, 'You treat your horse like you'd treat your own child, and it'll never turn against you.' So I'm gonna be kind and gentle with Moncado. I'll not expect him to act up, and he won't. Wait and see."

Lucie-Marie was happy to ride Tallulah, because she knew Annie Sharon had trained her well. But she worried for her sister. She worried about what Tie-Down would say. But she knew when an idea got into Annie Sharon's head, there was no stopping her.

When Annie Sharon started to saddle Moncado, the horse resisted a bit, but Annie Sharon remained firm, all the while talking sweet nothings to Moncado. Finally, the horse stood absolutely still while Annie Sharon finished tightening the belt under his belly. "Now, see, Lucie-Marie, that wasn't so bad," Annie Sharon said with some relief.

Now, only the trick of getting astride Moncado remained. Annie Sharon knew her body was built like Twanda's, so Moncado might find her body familiar. She mounted the frisky animal with no problems. She turned to Lucie-Marie and said confidently, "Let's go. We've got us a grand opening to ride in."

Off the two sisters and their horses trotted. Annie Sharon experienced the most peculiar sensation on the back of her mother's horse. She felt Twanda's voice comin' out of her mouth, singing quietly to Moncado, whispering to him, and soothing him. She was certain every time she opened her mouth, she sounded like her mother. Annie Sharon was full of a closeness to her mother she had not felt in years. The farther she rode Moncado, the closer the spirit of Twanda came, until Annie Sharon was ready to weep for joy. Her mama was not gone; she lived in her daughter's memories of her. Tears flooded Annie Sharon's eyes.

Lucie-Marie was about to ask what Annie Sharon thought their father would say when he found Annie Sharon atop Moncado, but her sister's confidence erased that thought for a moment. Tie-Down could get beside himself at the drop of a hat. Or the drop of a pin, for that matter. Lucie-Marie crossed herself and followed Annie Sharon's lead to the gathering spot for the Grand Opening of the Diamond-L Championship Rodeo.

Mr. Stephens began his entrance with the flag bearers before the girls were in line. With his empty sleeve blowing in the wind, he guided his horse to the center of the arena. Big Al rode behind him. The rest of the cowboys and cowgirls fell in line and made a circle of the arena three times while the crowd in the bleachers cheered them on. The customary singing of "The Star-Spangled Banner" and the Negro National Anthem, "Lift Every Voice and Sing," followed. Mr. Stephens led everyone in the Cowboy's Prayer. The riders circled the arena once more, and the time came for the rodeo to begin.

Tie-Down looked for his girls, but he did not catch sight of them until "the bombs bursting in air." He knew he could not be seeing right:

Annie Sharon sat atop Moncado. Nobody could ride that horse. He knew that for a fact. But there sat Annie Sharon just as calm and in control as her mama would have been. Tie-Down said, "Whoa," to his own horse and sat trying to decide how he could get through the hundreds of people in the arena to pull his daughter down and knock some sense into her. He felt a rush of blood through his head. A roaring in his ears shut out the voices of the people in the arena. His nails dug into the palms of his hands.

"Isn't that Annie Sharon on Moncado?" Cassie's voice, shrill and high-pitched, seemed to drift to Tie-Down through a rumble of thunder. "Tie-Down, get her off that dangerous animal!"

"Oh no. This can't be." Tie-Down's clenched fists shook. "She's got more brains than that. When I get her home, I'm gonna beat some sense into her head. That's the horse that killed her mother." The roaring in his ears grew louder, while angry tears blurred his vision.

chapter 4

Annie Sharon's eyes roved the crowd of faces, all topped with cowboy hats. Her father's face was somewhere among them, but where? She tugged lightly on Moncado's reins to turn him about, and he responded with short snorts and an anxious, prancing gait. Annie Sharon whispered and crooned to the horse, praising him for following her instructions so well. She told him he was a wonderful, fine animal. She explained that Twanda would be so very proud of him if she were there. She urged Moncado along as she looked for her father.

Moncado allowed her to steer him through the crowd, but his manner remained edgy and ill at ease.

Annie Sharon let out a loud sigh when she spotted Tie-Down. The sigh signaled both relief and anticipation. She rode Moncado through the other horses and riders to Tie-Down, sure he would be proud of her, pleased that his oldest demonstrated a courage to ride the horse nobody else on his ranch dared to ride.

But as she rode closer, she saw Tie-Down's face and sensed the anger bubbling inside him.

He rode to meet her, forcing his way through other competitors who moved aside when they noticed the scowl on his face. When he reached Annie Sharon, he leaped from his horse, reached up, and dragged her from Moncado's back. "Girl, don't you know you just about gave me a heart attack? What made you want to ride Moncado of all the horses we brought here? You know Moncado don't take to new riders. He's dangerous!"

The horse pranced about, his reins hanging free. Tie-Down snatched them, and held them clenched in a fist.

"But, Daddy, I thought you'd be proud of me," Annie Sharon whispered in a soft, apologetic voice. She looked at the people surrounding them, embarrassed and angry to find her father treating her like a small child. But she continued, "Moncado and me understand each other. I was easy with him. He started out a little nervous, but he was just gettin' used to the feel of me sittin' on his back."

"The horse was nervous?" Tie-Down asked. "What about me? Your mama died fallin' under that horse. You think I want to lose my daughter to that ornery critter, too?" Tie-Down held Annie Sharon's upper arms in a tight grip as she squirmed and blushed because of the pain.

Cassie pushed her way through the throng of riders lined up for the parade. She drew her horse, Liberty, along behind her, while Lucie-Marie led Tallulah and struggled to keep up. Cassie arrived to find Tie-Down flushed with rage, his arms stiff and straight, almost lifting Annie Sharon off the ground. Cassie talked to Tie-Down softly as she used her fingers to pry his hands from his daughter's arms.

"Okay, turn her loose, Tie-Down. You're hurting her."

After a few seconds, Tie-Down turned to look

at Cassie. He allowed her to wedge her body between him and Annie Sharon, staring at Cassie as if he had never seen her before.

But she whispered to him and cooed to him, much like Annie Sharon talked to Moncado. Tie-Down's eyes finally seemed to focus on Cassie's face. He struggled to regain his composure.

"Did you see what this fool girl did?" he asked Cassie.

"Oh, Daddy, I wasn't tryin' to upset you. I wanted to show you what a good horsewoman I am. That's all."

"Let's discuss it later," Cassie said. "Not here. Not now. You okay, girl?" Cassie asked.

"Yeah, I'm fine." Annie Sharon turned her head away. Her voice came out low and raspy.

Tie-Down said, "She's fine, but she's not gonna try anythin' like that again." He pushed his hat back on his head and wrapped one of his hands around the other to form one giant fist. He held his hands that way, tight, as if he was afraid of what they might do.

"But you were proud of me, weren't you, Daddy?" Annie Sharon asked.

Lucie-Marie looked on, but said nothing. Her focus shifted to Cassie, who was trying to settle Liberty down in the excitement of all the other horses and riders around them.

"Well, I'll tell you, Annie Sharon, this was no time for pride. I would never have believed you'd do this without askin' me. This is not somethin' Twanda would want to see you do, either. You're still just a slip of a girl; you got plenty of time to be a great horsewoman like your mama."

Talk of Twanda made Cassie a bit uneasy, but before she could deal with her inner feelings, Cassie noticed Lucie-Marie on Tallulah. Too late she remembered she had promised Liberty as Lucie-Marie's mount for the day. *How did I forget?* she asked herself. *I intended to have Tie-Down suggest a horse for me, but we got to talkin' about other things, and the horse slipped my mind. Oh, no.* Cassie knew one of the worst things to do to young people was to promise them something and then renege on that promise. Lucie-Marie made a point of not looking Cassie directly in the eye. She and Tallulah remained a good distance away as the others wrestled with the problem of Annie Sharon placing herself in grave danger.

"Lucie-Marie, I'm so sorry. I forgot I tol' you Liberty was yours for the day. Maybe we could trade. I'll ride Tallulah, and you can still have Liberty for the barrels."

Annie Sharon overheard them and rolled her eyes at Lucie-Marie, indicating Cassie would not be riding Tallulah. That was just too much to ask. First the woman wanted to take her mother's place. Now she wanted to ride Annie Sharon's horse.

Lucie-Marie said, "Naw, that's all right, Cassie. We brought a few other horses. And since Annie Sharon can't have Moncado, she'll pick another horse."

Tie-Down missed most of the conversation between the women in his life. The bustle of horses and riders preparing for the rodeo to start kept his mind strictly on business.

"C'mon, y'all. We gotta make sure Dupree has those calves in the chutes, ready for the calf-ropin' and the tie-down competition. Y'all will have plenty of time for chitchat later."

How Tie-Down could call their minimal conversation with Cassie chitchat was beyond Annie Sharon, but she understood her father's seriousness about business. And rodeo livestock accounted for the bulk of their business, so she did not say a word. She followed her father to the corrals, holding the steers, calves, and horses.

Tie-Down found Dupree in his chaps and ten-gallon hat sitting on a fence. "Are we ready to boogie?" Tie-Down asked.

"You bet we are," Dupree answered. "I'll get the calves in the chutes for the ropin'."

The calves moved through the mazes of wooden fences that led toward the arena until Tie-Down and Dupree felt satisfied they had enough for several riders.

"All right, Dupree, you can go tell Mr. Stephens we're ready here."

Dupree jumped on the back of his roan mare and rode over to the grandstand tower where the announcers and timekeepers waited for word on the status of the animals.

"We're set down here!" Dupree shouted.

Mr. Stephens looked down from the tower and

said, "'Bout time. I been ready to announce calf-ropin' for a while now." Over the loudspeaker, he announced, "Ladies and gentlemen, children of all ages, we're ready for our first event, calf-ropin'. You're gonna see some of the finest cowboys and cowgirls of East Texas and from around the world. Let's give 'em a big hand, okay? First up is Johnnie Maddox, a fine young cowboy, come all the way from Abilene to entertain you today. He's ropin' calf number twenty-four from Tie-Down Brown's herd of fiesty, ornery critters. Are you ready at the chute?"

Dupree waved his arm, signaling "Yes."

Johnnie Maddox sat on his horse in one chute with a calf in the chute next to him. With lightning-flash speed, the gates of both chutes opened. Out ran the calf. Out rode Maddox with a rope dangling from his mouth and a lasso swirling in the air. Soon the lasso settled around the calf's neck. Maddox leaped to the ground, and raised a hand to his horse. The horse halted, all four feet braced firmly on the ground, allowing just the amount of leverage to the rope that Maddox needed. Maddox picked the calf up and threw him to the ground. He grabbed the rope from his mouth and tied three legs of #24 together. He jumped away with his arms raised in the air, letting the crowd and the timekeepers know he succeeded. He removed his lasso from the calf's neck and the rope from the calf's legs. He headed back to his horse, an excellent roping horse by any standard. Maddox remounted his horse, and the calf ran off toward a chute that would take him out of the arena.

A smattering of applause rose from the fans in the grandstand. They knew the cowboys got the prizes, but the horses were as much a part of the victories as the cowboys' skills. The horses must serve as perfect partners in all of the rodeo events, or the cowboys might as well not show up.

The voice of the announcer boomed across the stands, "Maddox wrapped that little calf up in seven-point-one seconds, ladies and gentlemen. Let's hear it for the cowboy from West Texas."

Maddox dusted himself off and headed for the fence.

The lineup continued, and Tie-Down kept

listening for Cassie's name. He wished she would give up this idea of calf-roping, but that did not seem likely. She loved this business. Maybe as much as he did.

The next couple of cowboys after Maddox did not even rope the calf, so there was no chance of their tying the calf up. The crowd found this amusing. Mr. Stephens said in a kindly voice that these cowboys were not having much luck on this fine summer day.

A cowboy from Edna in South Texas was the next roper out of the chute. He finished in five seconds. That would be a rough standard to beat.

Finally, Cassie was up. She asked the spirits to be with her, and she talked to Liberty. "Liberty, we can do this. Don't you let me down now."

Liberty itched to get out of her chute as much as calf #47 wanted to get out of his holding pen. The chutes went up. Cassie heard the blur of Mr. Stephens's voice describing her actions. She and Liberty worked like a well-oiled machine as Cassie's rope settled around the calf's neck. Liberty stood her ground, but the calf's resistance to having its legs tied was ferocious. When Cassie finished, she heard, "Six seconds for the young cowgirl from Houston. Let's hear it, folks, for a fine cowgirl. One of the best scores we've had today from anybody, let alone a cowgirl. Let her know you care."

A tremendous yelping and applause from the crowd followed. Cassie retrieved her ropes and watched the pickup riders guide the calf to the other end of the arena. She somehow found herself atop Liberty again. She doffed her white hat at the folks in the stands, surprised the event had gone by so fast. She smiled, knowing she held a good chance of placing second in roping.

When she reached the open field, Cassie found Tie-Down waiting for her with obvious pride in his eyes. He tried to grab her up in his arms, but their horses stood in the way. They settled for a quick kiss.

"Cassie, you almost took my breath away. You were all over that calf, girl. I'm tellin' you, you were a sight to see. Any other day, and you'd have placed first. I know it in my bones."

Cassie tried not to show her disappointment at not placing first, but she could not hide that from Tie-Down.

"Hey, there'll be lots of other rodeos. The season ain't but half through, baby. Remember that."

"Well, I just hope that guy from Edna doesn't show up next time, is all." Cassie headed for the truck to let Liberty rest before the barrel races began, and because she wanted to watch the bareback riders.

Dupree was on the case for the bareback riders; the riders were ready, too. For this event, the horses and the cowboys entered the arena together from the same chute. The timekeeper started his count as soon as the first cowboy was seated on the back of an unbroken horse. With one arm in the air and the other holding onto the tether, the cowboy had to stay on the bronco for at least eight seconds. A lot of cowboys found themselves on the ground long before the time allotment. The pickup cowboys worked in the arena to guide the wild horses away from riders as quickly as possible so the riders didn't become trampled under horses' hooves.

Lucie-Marie watched Bo-Beep, in his silver and black, chasing broncs away from the cowboys who had been thrown before the clock ticked off the seconds. Other pickup boys rescued the riders. A few cowboys bit the dust before anyone reached the eight-second goal, and often trouble arose getting the cowboy to safety, because the wild horse was so out of control. In each instance, Bo-Beep came to the rescue.

Annie Sharon took a special interest in bareback, not only because of her mother, whom the pickup cowboys were unable to help, but also because of Diamondback. This was his biggest and best event. The horse he drew, #39, kicked up a storm while still in the corral. The cowhands struggled to hold him so Diamondback could get situated on his back. When the chute opened and the clock started, the horse bolted out. Diamondback seemed to float atop the horse, gliding as if on water. The horse tried to throw Diamondback off by arching its back and springing high into the air. It landed on its front feet and kicked its hind feet high into the air. Diamondback stayed on for the eight-second bell, and more. But he discovered he could not get off. Bo-Beep could not get there fast enough. As the horse bucked, Diamondback began to teeter to one side of the animal, his torso springing like a top on the right side of #39.

When Bo-Beep couldn't get there, Dupree jumped on his roan to help get Diamondback off that crazy horse. Annie Sharon thought she was going to faint or stop breathing. Why did the folks she loved feel like they had to ride these wild horses? Couldn't they see what it did to her? Finally, Dupree got to Diamondback just before he fell under the thrashing legs of #39.

Annie Sharon heard herself let out a scream. Diamondback's arm had become entangled in the tether to the horse. All three—Dupree, Diamondback, and Bo-Beep—gyrated in a mad, wild dance, struggling to get Diamondback undone and safe.

The crowd grew hushed. This was how cowboys became injured. Dupree, who usually took everything so easy, worked hard to free Diamondback. Once he had the boy safely on the roan, the crowd went mad with clapping and shouting for the pickup guys and Diamondback, who had never let loose of #39 throughout this ordeal.

Not more than a minute had passed, but Diamondback gave a sigh of relief that his eight seconds, and more, on that man-hating animal were over.

Annie Sharon felt like all of the life was drained out of her. She ran to Diamondback and Dupree and gave them each a big hug. She let herself be scooped up in Diamondback's long arms. She knew he had been more nervous than he wanted anyone to know. His shirt, now completely wet, stuck to his body and sweat streamed down his face.

Bo-Beep teased, "Ain't nothin' at all wrong with that boy. Why you treatin' him like he's a chile or somethin'? Annie Sharon, you know better than that!"

Annie Sharon flashed a grin at Bo-Beep. "I'm just checkin' to make sure you brought him back same as he was when he left."

Dupree disappeared into the corrals again, as if he preferred the company of animals to that of humans. He did have a way with animals, though, Annie Sharon thought. Nobody could deny that.

"Hey, Annie Sharon, don't you worry about me. I'm all right. Nothin's wrong with me. But barrels are next. You got to get ready, don't you?" Diamondback asked.

"Oh, Diamondback, I know what I gotta do. I just wanted to make sure you were all right. I'm ridin' Moncado, you know? Daddy got mad at me this morning for ridin' him in the parade, but Cassie calmed Daddy down; you know how he is with that woman. But I know I can handle Moncado. I'm trying so hard to make Daddy proud of me. I'm gonna try Moncado on the barrels; what do ya think? He's just right now gettin' used to me. Is it too soon to race him?"

"You sure your daddy's gonna stand for this? I don't think so, myself."

"He's gonna scream and yell, but it'll be too late then. My mama won all sorts of trophies with this horse, and I know he's still got winning in his bones. I just need a chance to show what I can do with him."

"Okay. If you're determined, just keep talkin' to him the way you been doin'. The pickup boys'll be right there. I don't mean no disrespect, but Moncado looks like he could outdo Tallulah without even breakin' a sweat," Diamondback said.

"Watch what you say about my horse, now," Annie Sharon snapped.

Lucie-Marie chimed in, "Yeah, watch what you say, 'cause Tallulah's carryin' me to victory this afternoon."

Big Al's booming voice cut all conversation short. Over the loudspeaker he announced a break for lunch.

While the cowhands set up big, empty oil barrels for the upcoming barrel races, the hundreds of spectators drifted out of the stands and milled about like an army of ants. The air almost crackled with excitement about the next event, but the aroma of barbecue drifted about the field, drawing the people away. They filled the seats at the picnic tables outside where others had eaten earlier. They spread blankets under shade trees and opened picnic baskets. And, of course, they visited the food stands Big Al provided.

Both Lucie-Marie and Annie Sharon were signed up for barrels. Both rode formidable horses today that could run barrels in their sleep, though Moncado had not raced in many years. The rivalry was on. Both of Twanda's sweethearts might distinguish themselves that afternoon. But right now, Diamondback wanted to go pick up his prize money. Annie Sharon went along with him. She had been terribly frightened for him, but now she felt equally proud that her fella stayed the course and rode the devil out of that crazy animal.

Rosie M. caught up with them. "You might as well enjoy helpin' Diamondback pick up his money," Rosie M. said, "'cause *you're* not pickin' up any money today. I'm gonna wipe you out, girl."

Annie Sharon laughed with her friend, who really could run some barrels. She knew Rosie M. was not talking out of her head, now. She could put her money where her mouth was. "We'll see, Rosie M. That's all I gotta say. We'll see."

The sounds of the rap group Mos Def blasted through the speakers. Big Al knew that to keep

the young folks involved, their music prefer-
ences and their dancing should be respected.
Cheers went up from unexpected places
around the arena and from the picnic tables
outside.

Rosie M. snapped her fingers and bopped up
and down in her saddle. Then just as everyone
was getting warmed up, the music switched to
Linda Ronstadt and Aaron Neville singing a
ballad. Big Al was not a successful rodeo pro-
ducer for no reason. He did his best to have a
little something for everybody. He even had an
old retired bull that mothers could pose their
toddlers on wearing cowboy garb, to look like
they were steer-riding. Big Al could be counted
on to find a way to make a buck. His next
event, barrel racing, was a big moneymaker,
even if it was a sport mostly participated in by
women. Participation was always high for this
event.

After he gave folks ample time to socialize
and savor his bar-be-cue, Big Al signaled to
Mr. Stephens that it was time for the barrel
racing to start.

"Ladies and gentlemen, please take your

seats. The beautiful cowgirls we've got here today are going to demonstrate their skills at racing barrels in just a few minutes. These are some of the prettiest and fastest women you're ever likely to see. So let's get ready to give them a round of applause."

Folks started to make their way back to their seats in the stands. Barrel racing was a favorite event for women of all ages: grandmas to granddaughters. The fans loved to watch the speed and finesse with which the women and their horses excelled.

"First up, we got a Ms. Angie Ramirez of Conroe, Texas. Let's hear it for Angie, folks."

A scattering of applause followed. The crowd needed time to focus its attention. Angie Ramirez waited atop her horse for a signal from the timekeeper. When Mr. Stephens waved an arm for the race to begin, Angie galloped off, her legs splayed in the stirrups, beating against the sides of her horse. She held her rope with both hands until she reached the first barrel in the cloverleaf pattern. She slowed her horse, and used her hand nearest the barrel to guide her horse around it. They circled the barrel with Angie failing to leave enough space between the horse's body and the barrel. The barrel toppled over, costing Angie a penalty of five seconds, to be subtracted from her final score.

They raced across to the second barrel. This time Angie used her leg nearest the barrel to nudge her horse to within about four feet of the barrel as they leaned their inside shoulders toward the barrel. This time they circled the barrel cleanly, and raced off to the final of the three barrels. They whipped around it and, too late, they sped off toward the gate from which they entered the arena. Angie's horse could not gallop fast enough to make up for the time lost by not hugging the barrels in the turns and the penalty, too.

"Angie Ramirez: twenty-three-point-six seconds. Better luck next time, Angie. Let's all rally for this young cowgirl from Conroe, folks. Next, we have Lucie-Marie Johnson-Brown from Houston, Texas. Sure you ready, Lucie-Marie?"

Lucie-Marie nodded. The flag came down. Lucie-Marie rode for the right barrel first, coming around at such a close angle she had to adjust her leg to make sure no part of her body, or Tallulah's, touched the barrel. She bolted across the arena to the second barrel in the blink of an eye. Around she went, as close as she could get, with Tallulah following her lead and working with her the whole time. The closer they rounded the barrels, the less time they lost. Lucie-Marie talked to Tallulah and kicked up around the third barrel.

She reached the finish line at such a pace she left a whirlwind of dust behind her.

"Lucie-Marie Johnson-Brown: ten-point-twenty-two seconds. What a ride this cowgirl gave us. Let's hear it for Lucie-Marie, folks."

All of Lucie-Marie's friends and competitors smiled at her as she left the arena; she had done a magnificent job. Tie-Down and Cassie waited for her, too.

"You rode that animal like all get-out, Lucie-Marie. I didn't know you had it in you," Tie-Down said. "I didn't know you were ridin' Tallulah."

"Yeah, Lucie-Marie, you were a sight for sore eyes. My heart was leapin' for joy when you came across the finish," Cassie added.

"Annie Sharon's got some sho' enough ridin' to do now," Tie-Down said, hugging his youngest daughter.

But Annie Sharon's name appeared much farther down the lineup of barrel racers. She had to wait for a bunch of competitors to ride before her: Agnes Gimene, thirteen-point-four; Sally Johnson, twelve-point-five; Louisiana Red, fourteen-point-seven; Rosie M., eleven-point-four. That meant the score Annie Sharon must beat was held by her sister. This did not set too well with Annie Sharon, who boasted so much about her own talents. Today the tables were turned. Lucie-Marie held the score to match.

Because of the number of barrel racers, Mr. Stephens divided them into two groups. One group performed before the "head and heel" event, and the second group went on before applied wrestling.

Head and heel involved a duo of cowboys. One cowboy threw a rope around the horns or head of a steer, and the second rider lassoed its back legs. If the cowboy managed to get a noose around only one leg, a five-second penalty applied. When both back legs were captured in the noose, somebody called "time." And the event ended.

Diamondback and his friend, Black Boo, earned a second place in "head and heel." So off Diamondback went with Annie Sharon, one more time, to pick up money. He felt he was having a fine day.

Annie Sharon felt as if her time to ride would never come. She had been at the rodeo most of the day and had yet to show her talents to the fine folks of East Texas. Annie Sharon and Diamondback made their way back to the arena as the second round of barrels started. Annie Sharon was so involved with Diamondback that she did not hear her name called at first.

"Let's welcome Ms. Annie Sharon Johnson-Brown from Houston. C'mon, Annie Sharon," Big Al announced.

Diamondback heard her name called and told it was time to go. A bit discombobulated, Annie Sharon made her way to the starting line on Moncado. She knew in her heart she would beat everybody. No way Moncado would let her down. When Mr. Stephens waved the starting flag, Moncado shot out into the arena, but he did not want to race around the first barrel. He seemed to want to run in a straight line. Annie Sharon fought against Moncado's instincts, trying to force him with her body to move tight around the barrels so she would make good time. But, instead of following Annie Sharon's lead, Moncado ran out of control all about the arena, finally rearing up on his back legs, his forearms and cannon bones making wild designs in the air.

Annie Sharon kept talking to her mount, "Moncado, hush, hush, now. Listen to me, stop!" She pulled the reins to bring pressure against Moncado's mouth, but to no avail. Suddenly she felt herself being lifted off Moncado. She looked around and found herself in the arms of pickup cowboy Bo-Beep.

Moncado kept kicking aimlessly in the air. He neighed and snorted. Dupree ran across the soft dirt as fast as he could. He jumped on the horse and rode him, as wild as he was acting, into an open chute.

When Bo-Beep set Annie Sharon down, she

shook her head, more stunned than frightened. She had never lost control of a horse before, but now she knew deep down, she should have listened to her father. Moncado had not been in competition since her Mother died. What could have been on her mind? She knew better. And Tie-Down would kill her for sure. How had she gotten herself into this mess? She had only defied him because she knew his chest would almost burst with pride if she proved she could ride her mother's horse.

Anyway, she needed him to notice her, to remember his daughters. Since Cassie came into his life, he walked around in a fog, noticing no one else. She closed her eyes to block out the memory of his kissing Cassie in the kitchen last night.

Searing pain spread down one of her thighs, so intense it brought tears to her eyes. She opened them to answer Bo-Beep, who still sat with her on a bench in the barn, asking how she felt. "I'm fine," she lied. To herself she thought: I'm just so embarrassed I could die.

"You all right, Annie Sharon?" It was her father's voice, angry, and disappointed, and worried. "What am I doin' wrong where you're concerned? What got into you to make you do this fool thing?" He nodded his head toward Bo-Beep, and the pickup cowboy stood up and trotted back to the arena, glancing once over his shoulder at the father and daughter.

"Okay," Tie-Down said. "We talked about that fool horse this mornin'. I thought we both understood he's a killer." Tie-Down's voice shook. He clasped his hands together again as if he were afraid of what they might do unless he controlled them. "How come I didn't know you planned to ride this horse again? You used to talk to me and tell me what you had troublin' you inside."

"Oh, Daddy. I can't get you to see me anymore. You spend all your time with Cassie. I don't want Cassie in our house. I want things like they used to be, with you, Mama, Lucie-Marie, and me." Tears slid down Annie Sharon's face.

"Forget that kind of talk, girl. We don't have that no more." Tie-Down pulled Annie Sharon up from the bench, and awkwardly wrapped his arms around her. She leaned against him, sobbing.

Cassie rode over to Tie-Down and his

daughter with Lucie-Marie, Rosie M., and Diamondback in tow. "I could take a look at you, Annie Sharon. Sometimes you can't tell you're injured after a crazy horse has gone buck wild on you. We could take you over to the medics?" Cassie touched Annie Sharon's shoulder.

"Naw, naw. Y'all stop botherin' after me. I'm just fine, and at least we got one champion today." Annie Sharon swiped at her tears and tried to smile. "Lucie-Marie, you had a great run," she complimented her sister.

"Tallulah was fabulous. You trained her good, Annie," Lucie-Marie said.

"But you the one that rode her, Lucie-Marie. You take credit for yourself, you hear me?" Annie Sharon wrinkled her brow at her sister. She winced in pain, a movement Cassie picked up on immediately. So did her friends and her father.

"We're going to the medics," Cassie said, and this time Annie Sharon did not protest. When a cart arrived to transport her, Diamondback helped her in.

An awkward silence followed before Tie-Down said, "Well, we ain't nowhere near settling the problem we got here. But I got me one steer to wrestle. I could skip that and go with you, Annie Sharon."

"We'll be fine," Cassie said.

Ten minutes later, the situation did not look so good after all. The medics tended the sprained muscle in Annie Sharon's leg, but promised that several days of careful activity would make her as good as new.

Meanwhile, Tie-Down knew all of the bulls in the competition well; they came from his ranch. But he did not have a choice of which bull he would wrestle. He drew Madness, as rough a bull as anybody ever did see. Tie-Down's was the first name on the list, and he sat on his horse, tense and impatient, waiting for the signal that could send him to victory, or to injury, or worse.

First off, a cowboy called a "hazer" came into the arena to keep the steer from running away from the "doggers," the wrestling cowboys. On signal, Tie-Down burst from his chute on his horse, his black leather vest shining in the sun, and the long, leather fringes of his chaps swirling in the wind. The bull ran for all he was worth, with the hazer herding him in a straight line so Tie-Down could catch him.

When Tie-Down caught up to Madness, he slid from his horse and grabbed the bull's horns, forcing him to stop. He wrenched Madness's head to one side, dropped him to the ground, and made sure all four of his legs were off the ground. Only three-point-two seconds ticked away while Tie-Down achieved this task, which allowed him to claim first prize after all of the other competitors had their chances.

Tie-Down was lucky to get out of the ring. Two of the cowboys who bulldogged after him were gored and required tending at the local hospital. The rodeo medics could do nothing for them.

During the bull-riding competition, a bull threw Dupree off his back, breaking a few of Dupree's ribs, but the ranch manager drew second place money. The medics bound him up and told Dupree he should take it easy for a while and allow the ribs to heal.

So the Brown family, as a group, did not fare too badly. Only Annie Sharon did not place. But she knew other rodeos would provide other chances.

When the events of the day ended, Dupree

went to the truck to rest. Tie-Down and Cassie made sure the animals were watered and secured. She suggested Tie-Down talk to Annie Sharon about Moncado at another time with everyone using cooler heads. Then the two grown-ups rode off on their horses to the Silver Spur to eat supper and visit with their friends before the long trip home. The teenagers stayed in the arena to dance—girls to one side, boys on the other—while Big Al and Mama Big Al kept an eye on things, trying to shut their ears to the hard rhythm of hip-hop music.

chapter 5

The next day, Sunday, provided time to rest and visit with family and friends. Over a breakfast of ranchero eggs, ham, grits with cheese, and biscuits, Annie Sharon waited for her father to smack her for yesterday's behavior or to say she had made as good a meal as any grown woman could make, even her mother.

While Tie-Down ate, he thought about how he could have lost his oldest daughter in an accident on Moncado yesterday, how he would have to do something about that.

"Annie Sharon, these grits really stick to a man's ribs," he said.

"Glad you enjoyed them, Daddy." Annie Sharon beamed.

"Tell him I made the biscuits, Annie Sharon," Lucie-Marie blurted out.

Before Annie Sharon could answer, Tie-Down said, "Oh, Lucie-Marie, I could tell you made those biscuits. There was a touch of love in them, and that's your mark for sure."

"Really, Daddy, you could tell?"

"No doubt about it." Tie-Down smiled.

The three of them cleared the table. Tie-Down hesitated for a minute. "Annie Sharon, I'm gonna take a cup of coffee out on the porch; we've got some talkin' to do."

Her heart seemed to skip a beat. She had been surprised when her father did not mete out punishment last night for her disobedience. Cassie seemed able to keep Tie-Down's anger in check. *Might be good if she was here now. Where is she when you need her,* Annie Sharon wondered.

Lucie-Marie's disappointment that she was not invited was short-lived. She simply invited herself. "I'll bring more coffee out to you, Daddy."

Tie-Down strolled outside to a fresh country

morning. When his girls were going to stop vying for his attention was beyond him. He tried to treat them equally, but they were so different. He seldom knew if he was doing the right thing, but this morning he did not doubt himself. They both needed to hear what he needed to say.

First, he savored his coffee. Last month Cassie found him a special blend of fresh, ground coffee called Cowboy. He liked it, not only because of its strength and rich taste, but because Cassie took the trouble to look for it.

He settled in a porch rocker, with Lucie-Marie in the hammock and Annie Sharon at his feet. He began, "We learned a lot yesterday, girls."

"We did?" the girls asked in unison.

"Yep, we did," Tie-Down said. "We gotta animal that's runnin' wild."

"Oh." All that Annie Sharon could think about was what Tie-Down would do to her.

"Yeah, we gotta do somethin' about Moncado 'fore he kills somebody."

"But what can we do, Daddy? He's already set in his ways. Mama trained him good. I don't know what got into him yesterday," Annie Sharon's voice wavered the slightest bit.

"Your mama trained him to her likin', and Moncado listened to her, and her alone. That was selfish and dangerous. A horse shouldn't go wild when mounted by other riders. I warned her about that. Annie Sharon, you're just mighty lucky, is all I can say."

"You mean it wasn't my fault that Moncado wouldn't mind?"

"Absolutely not," Tie-Down replied gently, "though you never should've been on him."

"Well, what're we goin' to do?" Annie Sharon asked.

Lucie-Marie lay in the hammock listening, her eyes moving from her father to her sister and back again.

"We're goin' to retrain him, so that Moncado does everythin' you or any other rider asks him to do—if your leg's feeling up to it."

"We are?" Annie Sharon asked.

"Yep, and we're gonna start today. Leave those dishes till later, girls. I mean to get that animal on the right track this mornin'." Tie-Down rose from his chair and headed for the stables like a man possessed. "Let's get goin', girls. You both need to learn this. Annie Sharon, get that twelve foot lead rope and fasten it 'round Moncado, all the time talkin' sweet talk and lovin' him up. Then bring him on out to the corral."

While Annie Sharon hooked Moncado to the cloth rope used for training horses, Lucie-Marie listened to her father. He said, "You've got to earn your horse's trust and treat him like any good friend. Find out what moves him. Does he think the world is an okay place, or is he afraid?"

When Annie Sharon approached with Moncado following peacefully behind her, Tie-Down's voice grew more serious. "You gotta know why and how your horse responds to everythin', whether it's a raised hand, a loud truck, or a plastic bag blowin' in the wind. You need to know what frightens your animal before you get on his back. I like to think of every horse as a puzzle with at least one problem, maybe plenty more. Then I help him through them. But I must know what these problems are before they get me out on the prairie, and I've gotta long walk home, or worse."

Annie Sharon and Lucie-Marie listened without a word. Annie Sharon let out a sigh of
relief. Her father might not punish her for her
foolishness after all.

"You stay sensitive to your horse's emotions,
and constantly offer reassurance. That's how
you create a confident, trustin' partner. Now you
two come out from behind me. Annie Sharon,
you've got to deal with Moncado. Lucie-Marie,
you go get Tallulah. That's a horse that Annie
Sharon trained, and you've got to make that
horse your own if you want to ride her. Just like
she's gotta make her mama's horse hers."

Lucie-Marie ran off to fetch Tallulah. When
she returned, she found Tie-Down waiting,
ready for them both.

"Now what we wanna do is get your horse
thinkin' clear and logically while he walks
around you in a circle. Stand on the horse's
left side. Now run the lead rope under the
horse's neck, then reach over the horse's back
and take the rope in your right hand. Now, run
the rope 'round the horse's other side, then
behind the upper hind legs, well beneath the
dock of the tail."

The girls managed this easily enough, and waited for more instruction.

"Now move away from your horse, and ask him to unwind while you apply light pressure with the rope. This is goin' to teach the horse to move away from pressure, switch his eye contact with you from left to right and step over himself the right way. Now, when he comes out the other side, he'll start to move to the right. Lift your left arm to ask for movement again. If that doesn't work, Annie Sharon, you can slap your leg, cluck your tongue, or gently tap his behind with the end of your rope in a swingin' motion."

Tie-Down quieted and stepped back to watch his girls for a minute. He saw no problems, so he continued. "All right. Now do whatever it takes to get movement, but stop as soon as the animal does what you want. Drive the horse from behind, Lucie-Marie, keepin' a safe distance. Annie Sharon, keep away from the back legs, and give your rope some slack. Use the hand closest to your horse's mouth. That's right, use your right hand to hold the rope; grab the lead in an overhand so your little finger is nearest the head.

"Now, what you want, girls," Tie-Down continued, "is for these horses to move easily in a good, shaped circle with their bodies bendin' in an arc, like the circle. Lucie-Marie, if your horse slows down, use your left hand to accelerate, so pretty soon your horse will know a raised arm means for him to move. That's right . . . you're both doin' great.

"Annie Sharon, you can make your horse stop strayin' too close to you if you use your right palm, pushin' toward Moncado's eye. Bump his cheek if necessary. This ain't some silly exercise I'm showin' you two. You're teachin' your horse to drive and move forward at a particular speed. You're usin' your body language to tell the horse you want forward movement. Now, let's try a trot; then come back to a walk. Annie Sharon, this is so important for you and Moncado. It's necessary that when you ask him to go, he can think about it and go. He needs to walk with reasonable thinkin'. If Moncado's movements are really fast, sudden, and impulsive like they were yesterday, that's when he can get you into trouble on the saddle. But all that can be fixed on the ground. That's the point of this lesson. You understand, Lucie-Marie?"

Both girls nodded "Yes" and kept their horses movin' in circles around them until Tie-Down indicated it was wind-down time. He explained a one-rein stop to bring the horse back to its comfort zone. "Stroke them where they can be praised and stroked. Don't forget to stroke his flank and rib area, too. Keep a light feel to the rein on the horse's mouth, givin' when the horse gives. Say 'Whoa' if you need to, but eventually he'll stop. When he does, let go immediately, so he knows he's done what you wanted. Is all that clear to y'all?

"I've gotta go now; I got ranch work to do, so I can't stay through the afternoon. All your work's to be done on the ground. If you've got any questions or you feel your animal is challengin' you, ask Dupree for some help. He'll know what to do. Okay?"

"Yes, Daddy," both girls answered, though Annie Sharon was a bit put out that her father seemed to have forgotten the many lessons he gave them earlier in how to train a horse.

Tie-Down caught the defiance in her glance. "Don't roll your eyes at me, young lady. It wasn't my horse that refused to run barrels—wouldn't do anything you wanted, far as I could see."

Annie Sharon knew better than to say a word, especially since he was right. The girls spent the rest of the morning running Moncado and Tallulah through the motions their father showed them. But when the sun grew too hot and Annie Sharon's injured leg grew tired, she yelled for Dupree.

"Dupree, ain't it too hot to have these animals out here goin' in circles now?"

"It might be, if you fix me up some chicken fried steak this evenin'!"

The girls laughed. "Is that all it takes to get out from under this sun, Dupree?" Lucie-Marie asked.

"Well, you got yourself a deal," Annie Sharon quipped.

"But y'all gotta wash and brush those animals down, you hear me?"

The girls did not have to be told. They loved horses, loved treating them right with care and love. Some things they knew. Nobody needed to tell them.

Later in the day, the strains of zydeco music performed by Step Rideaux with its accordions, washboards, and violins drifted to the kitchen from Dupree's trailer. Annie Sharon peeked through the window over the sink and, sure enough, Dupree capered in the yard out there, dancing to the music of his people. He loved Creole zydeco.

So many Creoles and their descendants lived in East Texas that it was hard to believe this was not the state of Louisiana. The "Frenchmen," as the Creoles were called, had an impact on everything, from food to music.

Annie Sharon could make a good roux for gumbo or fry up tasty alligator meat, but Dupree had asked for chicken-fried steak, and that's what she would make for him.

She found it simple enough: dredge the steaks through a nicely seasoned flour, drop them in a pan of hot grease, and then remember to take the meat out before it got tough. Annie Sharon whipped up some sweet potatoes, dandelion greens, and corn bread, too. She felt generous. Diamondback had called, saying he would come by later in the evening to chat with her on the porch. That is, if Tie-Down agreed. Annie Sharon would make a good home-cooked meal to, hopefully, put her daddy in a really good mood.

Cassie was coming over, too. To Annie Sharon's surprise, she looked forward to Cassie's visit today almost as much as her father did. She wanted Cassie to read the Tarot again. Moncado's behavior at the rodeo vexed Annie Sharon and embarrassed her. She wanted to know what lesson she was meant to learn from that experience. Why did her mother train her horse in such a way that nobody else could ride him?

Maybe the Tarot would answer those questions. Her father certainly could not. Annie Sharon was surprised he had talked against her mother earlier about the horse. To him, nothing her mother ever did was wrong or careless. Twanda Rochelle Johnson-Brown was like a rodeo goddess to Tie-Down. But Annie Sharon was at a point where she really wanted to know what kind of woman her mother was. She wanted to know what Twanda would do with Moncado now if she were here.

What would she say about Diamondback? Was he going to be a good man for her, or not? This is what Annie Sharon wanted to know. What would Twanda say about her cooking? Simple little details, but she wanted the answers from her mama.

When Cassie arrived, Tie-Down was still out on the range mending fences, and Lucie-Marie was taking a nap on the sofa. Dupree's mood had changed to the blaring music of blues singer Mel Waiters and the country sounds of Reba McEntire. He still danced by himself, out near the corral, which made Cassie and Annie Sharon laugh.

"Dupree ever have himself a girlfriend?" Cassie asked Annie Sharon.

"Not as far as I know. He's all tied up with horses and steers. Says he doesn't have the temperament for a woman, but horses like him just fine."

Cassie thought about that for a minute and said, "Maybe it's for the best then. Save us womenfolk from one more bad experience."

Annie Sharon found herself enjoying Cassie's company. When she realized this, she felt awkward and self-conscious. She tried to restrain herself by directing a question to Cassie that would put a halt to all the gaiety. "Cassie, did you bring those Tarot cards?" Annie Sharon asked in a casual voice.

"Always," Cassie replied, bouncing up and down, still enjoying Dupree's music.

"Well, can you do a reading for me, then?"

"I guess we can. Smells like supper's ready, so we won't have to hurry. It's good we're alone, too. Tarot reading is very personal, Annie Sharon."

"Oh, I didn't know that," Annie Sharon.

"Now, don't let that put you off none. No matter who else is around, your experience of the cards is personal. Nobody will understand what's revealed, but you." Cassie drew the cards from her purse. No words were exchanged between the two until the last card lay face-up.

Cassie said, "Uhmmm, that makes sense."

Annie Sharon jumped. "What makes sense?"

"Well . . . that the Hermit showed up, is what."

"Why? What's going on about this 'hermit'?"

Cassie put her hand over her mouth to cover a yawn and stretched her back. "It means that you're on a spiritual journey."

The two stared at each other, with Cassie not understanding that Annie Sharon had no idea what Cassie was trying to tell her.

"Please tell me what that means!" Annie Sharon said, frustration obvious in her voice.

"Means you've got a path to follow before the answer'll come, is what."

"What path? What journey?" Annie Sharon asked. "I thought you could help me."

"It's not me; it's your path that will help you. All I can do is help you see it."

Annie Sharon grew impatient. "Then what am I sposed to see?"

Trying to calm her, Cassie said, "Well, look at this. There's the Five of Pentacles starin' you right in the face."

"And what does that mean?" Annie Sharon asked.

"Means you're at the water's edge."

"Now you're losin' me again. What water's edge?"

Cassie thought for a moment, sucked her teeth, and breathed deeply. Finally, she told Annie Sharon, "You've got some waters to cross 'fore anythin' will make any sense to you."

Fed up with this talk, Annie Sharon stood up and moved away from the table, rubbing her forehead. "You just don't get it, Cassie. I'm tryin' to find out how to live my life and you're talkin' to me about some water."

"Not just any water, Annie Sharon. Might not be water you can see. Might just be how you feel, like you're movin' through water, or tryin' to swim against the current. Somethin' like that. You know what I mean?" Cassie waited for Annie Sharon to answer or question, but she experienced only silence for a time.

Then the girl said, "We ain't got no runnin' stream; we got a lake."

With that, Cassie's eyes lit up. "We got it! We got it. Annie Sharon, lookie here. There's the Heirophant. He means we're goin' to meet a preacher or a seer, somebody who'll know which path you're to take. Now's the time for us to go see the other women of my tribe."

Annie Sharon stared at her. "There you go with that 'tribe' stuff again."

Cassie smiled. "Yes, my tribe."

Annie Sharon challenged Cassie, "Well, if you got a 'tribe,' why you so colored?"

Without batting an eye, Cassie answered, "'Cause part of my tribe is 'colored,' too, if you wanna put it that way. But you'll see when we go out to the reservation."

"You mean a real Indian reservation?"

"No, Annie Sharon, an Apache reservation."

"Well, that's all right, I guess. I mean, that might seem like somethin' we could do. But I think the cards are sayin' somethin' different to me. Can you tell me again, real quick, what they tol' us?"

"Certainly," Cassie said. "Now, what we've got here are the Five of Pentacles, the Hermit, and the Hierophant."

"So, that's what we've got, huh?"

"Yep, that's it."

"And they're all sayin' that I'm on a journey, and that I'm lookin' for someone or somethin' to give me direction, right?"

"For the most part, that's what they say."
Cassie nodded her head.

"Well, you know what I think, Cassie?"

"Not unless you tell me," Cassie said.

"I don't think we're supposed to run off to
the reservation. No offense, now. But I think
my mama's tryin' to tell me to pay attention to
somethin'. I just don't know what." Annie
Sharon stood up, yawning, and walked away.

"Where you goin'? Ain't you goin' to serve up
supper?" Cassie asked as Annie Sharon disappeared into the house.

"Naw, you do it," Annie Sharon shouted. She
wished Twanda could tell her the things she
wanted to know. Suddenly a deep sadness filled
her, and she needed to be alone. By the time
Annie Sharon got to her bedroom, she found
herself awash in tears. She cried so hard, her
breath caught in her throat. Something that felt
huge churned in her stomach. She had no idea
where the tears came from and had no power to
stop them. She screamed, "Mama, why? Mama,
come back to me." She wept because she held a
clear vision of her mother in her mind, but
could not touch her. She thought she heard her

mother calling, but she could not tell where the voice came from. Certain she did not imagine the voice, her eyes frantically searched the room, wide and unblinking.

Annie Sharon's nose picked up Twanda's familiar scent of horse and perfume, but Annie Sharon could not find her. Am I going crazy? she asked herself. She felt as if she were being torn apart. Her mother was in her and yet not with her. Twanda's memory served as inspiration, but at the same time, as an emotional trap.

Sometimes when Annie Sharon thought about how much she missed her mother, she crawled into a corner, sitting there for hours, not speaking to a soul. Other times she thought of her mother and rushed off to ride Tallulah. She felt training Tallulah was a way to connect with Twanda.

Now Cassie had these cards that Annie Sharon knew in her bones her mother was using to reach her. But to say what to her? What did Twanda want her oldest girl to know? What was the journey?

On her bed now, Annie Sharon said aloud, "I should talk to Cassie some more. Find out from Cassie what Mama was like. She might tell me things Daddy never would. Maybe I can put Cassie's knowledge with her Tarot reading and come up with some answers. Find out what my mission is." She felt the muscles in her body relax, her breathing become even, and the tears subside. Annie Sharon's body relaxed. She fell into a deep sleep, peaceful as an infant in its mother's arms. And Twanda visited her daughter in her dreams.

"Look how beautiful everythin' is," Twanda said to her daughter. Hills rose from the earth like giant muscles. Annie Sharon and Twanda sat at the edge of Lost River, ready to ride Tallulah and Moncado along the banks to give the horses, and themselves, a little cooling off. Obviously, they had ridden hard. They were out of breath and glistening with sweat in the noonday heat. Twanda laughed for the pure joy of it. Annie Sharon blushed at her mother's ability to let loose, to be herself anywhere.

Twanda turned to Annie Sharon. "You're too young to be so serious, Annie. You need to let grown-up folks worry about grown-up things. Be a child while you can."

Annie Sharon wanted to tell her mother she would be more playful if she could actually let whimsy carry her away sometimes. But somebody had to look after Lucie-Marie and comb her hair, watch after the kinds of friends she made. And Tie-Down might never eat a decent meal if it were not for her.

"What are y'all up to?" Tie-Down teased. He appeared behind them from the hills. But Annie Sharon's attention remained on her mother.

"Listen to me," Twanda said. "Life takes care of itself. You're not responsible for them anymore, sweetie-pie. You never were, my dumplin'."

Cassie suddenly appeared next to Lucie-Marie, who practiced her roping tricks on horseback. With nothing more than a wave good-bye and a kiss thrown to Annie Sharon's cheek, Twanda vanished as mysteriously as she appeared.

Cassie, Lucie-Marie, and Tie-Down settled down to a picnic lunch on a patchwork quilt Twanda had made for Annie Sharon's bed. The quilt showed a Cherokee girl holding a basket of corn in the space left for Annie Sharon to sit. Cassie beckoned her to join them.

Tie-Down turned to Annie Sharon and said, "I want all the girls I love around me. C'mon, sweetie-pie."

Annie Sharon jumped off Moncado instead of her usual horse, Tallulah, to run to her father's side.

"I love you," Tie-Down whispered as he gave a flip to Annie Sharon's ponytail, the way her mother used to. Lucie-Marie and Cassie kept busy, eating. They didn't seem to notice anything.

"Annie Sharon! Annie Sharon, my vittles ready yet?"

Annie Sharon pulled herself away from the dream. Dupree's shout startled her and brought her back to the reality of the ranch house and the quiet of Sunday afternoon. She had forgotten about Dupree and his chicken-fried steaks. What else did she make for him? Oh, yes. Dandelion greens, sweet potatoes, and corn bread. She sighed; at least she had gotten that much done before she fell asleep. Now she needed to write down her dream, but that would have to wait. Somehow, Annie Sharon's heart felt lighter, her step quicker, her smile content as she headed out to the kitchen.

"Now, Dupree, you know I've got you covered." Dupree's music still blasted. Annie Sharon chuckled. "Some folks listen to classical music during dinner, Dupree. What's that you got playin'?"

Dupree laughed, too. He washed his hands with Borax to remove the usual dirt and grime he picked up working around the ranch. " 'She Thinks My Tractor's Sexy'; do you like it? How's your leg feeling?"

Annie moved among her simmering pots, her tasty bread, and her tea just begging for ice and lemons. "I'm okay," she said, hoping he would let the matter rest.

"You need any help, Annie Sharon?" Cassie asked.

"No thanks, Cassie. I'm doin' just fine, thank you." Then Annie Sharon hesitated. "But I'd appreciate some help tomorrow, all right?"

Cassie's eyes grew wide. "You bet!" she said.

"Annie Sharon, you don't ever let anybody in your kitchen," Lucie-Marie challenged.

"Well, things are goin' to change 'round here. Wait and see," Annie Sharon said.

When Tie-Down came in for supper, things quieted. Annie Sharon said the grace. "Lord, make us thankful for this food. Bless our bodies and spirits. This we ask in Jesus' name. Amen."

Tie-Down frowned. "That's not the way I taught you," he said.

"Yeah, but Cassie says we can bond with God in a personal way. We can even have conversation."

Tie-Down looked at Cassie. "You said that?"

Cassie lowered her eyes and toyed with the food on her plate. "Yeah, I might have said somethin' like that."

Tie-Down's brow knitted, but he tried to cover his displeasure. "Well, I wish you'd talked to me first."

Cassie looked him in the eyes and said, "Next time, I most certainly will."

Satisfied he and Cassie were of a like mind, Tie-Down asked the girls, "So how'd it go with you two after I left today?"

Lucie-Marie spoke up first, grinning. "Well, we kept the horses out till it just got too hot. And we thought, too, that Annie Sharon should get off her leg. But later this evening, after I had a nap, Dupree and I practiced my ropin' some more. Didn't we, Dupree? I really am gettin' good, Daddy. You know, I practiced lariats. That's really tricky stuff!"

"I'll say it is. Annie Sharon, did you train Tallulah any for that sort of thing?"

"No, she did not. I'll be training my own horse now," Lucie-Marie said, a twinkle in her eye.

"Darn, Lucie-Marie, you didn't even let me and Dupree get a word in," Annie Sharon said.

Dupree said, "Now, don't you two get to arguin' here. There's plenty enough talent to go 'round. And plenty of horses to work with."

Cassie asked, "Well, what did you and Moncado work on today?"

"I guess we worked on trustin' each other. Yeah, I think you could say that. Right, Daddy?"

Tie-Down pushed his plate away and sighed. "You sho' enough did work on trust. But remember that when a horse starts workin' its mouth, he's lettin' you know he's got your point. If you push a horse much beyond that, you're pushin' him away from you."

"Oh, I won't forget that, Daddy."

Dupree, quite pleased with his supper, chimed in, "One of these days I do believe I'm gonna see these girls doin' stunts in the Soul Circus."

Tie-Down's face went blank. "The circus? When was the last time you saw blacks in the circus?" Tie-Down asked.

"Last month, when a black circus came to town."

"He's right," Cassie said. "I tol' you about it—about how black performers from all over the world, like Kenya and Brazil, were in town doin' unbelievable stunts and acrobatics. All black folks."

"So now we got a circus, huh? Well, I want my girls to do more with their lives than perform tricks in a circus," Tie-Down said.

"What you got against a circus, boy?" Cassie asked, laughing. "Didn't we discuss that blacks since Bill Pickett have been performin' rope tricks and steer-doggin'? Besides, doin' one thing don't mean you can't do somethin' else. I'm a full-time surgical nurse, but I ride in rodeos."

"It ain't the same," Tie-Down began, but the ringing telephone interrupted him. "Annie

Sharon, get that, and remind whoever it is that I don't like gettin' calls during supper. It's the only time I got my family all to myself."

Annie Sharon rushed off to the phone, expecting a call from Diamondback.

The conversation continued at the table. "Well, it's not that I actually have anythin' against the circus, Cassie, it's just such a hard life. The rodeo, the circus. Either one is too hard for a woman. And believe me, I've spent a lot of time thinkin' about that since Twanda passed away." Tie-Down's voice trailed off as if he were thinking aloud.

"But what happened to Twanda could happen to anyone workin' a ranch; you know that."

"I guess I do," Tie-Down allowed. "I just don't want it to happen twice, is all."

"Well, we'll just train these girls so good that accidents will be as rare as bein' struck by lightnin'."

Tie-Down started to say something more, but before he could form the words, Dupree asked Annie Sharon, "Where's the fire, girl? You're gonna knock the dinner table over."

"Oh! I'm so happy. I might even kiss you, Dupree. Oh, Daddy! Daddy, I love you."

"Girl, what's got into you? I bet I know, though, so I'm not goin' to say another word. I'll let you do all the talkin'.". Tie-Down winked at Cassie.

"Daddy, Diamondback may invite me to go with him to the Triple-R Ranch when he and his dad come by tonight. Can you believe it? Can you believe it? The Triple-R."

"The Triple-R's got two arenas, don't it?"

"Yes, Daddy. One inside and the usual one outside."

"Well, what's so special about going out there?"

"Diamondback," Lucie-Marie squealed.

"You're too young to be keepin' company, Annie Sharon. You know that." Tie-Down left little room for Annie Sharon to negotiate or argue.

"It's not 'keepin' company,' Daddy. A whole bunch of us are gonna go. Isn't that right, Lucie-Marie?"

"Oh, yeah, a whole bunch of us. Me too."

"So now you think you're goin', too. This is really gettin' funnier by the minute."

"Tie-Down, why don't we find out what the girls'll be doin' at the Triple-R before you just say they can't go," Cassie suggested.

"We're gonna be ridin' horses, bar-be-cuein', dancin', stuff like that."

"Who's gonna be watchin' after y'all?"

"I guess Tookie's folks, since they own the place."

"Well, I gotta have more information than that. Get me the phone. I know Gene Barnes has got more on his mind than looking out after a passel of children."

"Daddy, you're gonna embarrass me!"

"Get the phone, or this conversation's over."

"Okay." Annie Sharon brought the phone to Tie-Down. "You'll make me look like a baby, though," she mumbled.

Cassie tried to ease the tension of the moment. "I remember ridin' with my friends when I was about your age. We had some great times. Tie-Down, didn't you ever spend afternoons with your friends during the summer?"

"Oh, yeah! That's why I'm callin' Gene now."

Cassie, Annie Sharon, and Lucie-Marie exchanged glances. Lucie-Marie crossed her fingers and held them where Annie Sharon could see them. Annie Sharon crossed her fingers, too. Then Cassie crossed her fingers, as Tie-Down dialed the Barneses' number.

"Hey, Gene, how you doin', man? Well, that's good to hear. What's this about you havin' a to-do for the kids next week? Oh, ho! Tookie's birthday, huh? A trail-ride, and food, and music sounds great. And you're expectin' my girls. Yeah, Cassie and I can stop by for a minute. But we already promised to play some dominoes at another friend's house. Wonderful! Around one o'clock? Okay, we'll see you then."

Tie-Down gave the phone back to Annie Sharon, who found it hard to come up with something to say.

"See there, girl, you didn't need no boy to invite you over to Tookie Barnes's. You were invited on your own. Lucie-Marie, too."

"So that means we can go, then?" Annie Sharon asked, her voice barely audible.

"Didn't you hear me tell Gene Barnes he'll see all of us early Saturday afternoon?"

The girls smiled and relaxed.

Cassie winked at them. She was impressed by Tie-Down's actions. It never hurt to know whom your children were with and what they would be doing. But this time Tie-Down was reasonable. At least he did not end the whole affair with an unexamined "No." Yeah, Tie-Down was starting to get a better hang of this parenting thing, she thought. She was quietly pleased that he included her in the activities, as well. She liked being a part of the family. A part of *this* family.

"Daddy, can we bring our own horses since you're goin', too?" Annie Sharon asked. "We could use our trailer and take Moncado and Tallulah, now that we're workin' with 'em."

"I don't see why not," Tie-Down said. The girls' excitement puzzled him. He didn't understand why they should be so overjoyed to see the same kids they saw yesterday. Things were so different when he was young. Girls were not nearly as involved in the rodeo or around boys when boys were with their horses. Girls spent more of their time in the kitchen or on the porch, not in the rodeo arena. But, as Cassie reminded him on a daily basis, times changed.

"Hey, Annie Sharon, what're we goin' to give Tookie for her birthday?" Lucie-Marie asked. "Shouldn't we go shoppin'? Cassie, will you take us to The Galleria to get a present for Tookie? Please?"

Annie Sharon watched Cassie carefully, waiting for her answer.

"Of course I will, but we better get a move on. It closes early today."

"Oh, boy. Dupree, we gotta practice some ropin' tricks later. You'll help me?"

Dupree nodded. "First, I'm gonna go rest awhile—encourage my ribs to heal."

"Since all y'all got somethin' to do, I'm gonna take me a nap, and let this delicious supper digest," Tie-Down said.

"Okay, spoilsport. We'll handle the shopping, won't we, girls?" Cassie asked.

"Yes, Cassie." The girls echoed each other.

"I know just what to get Tookie, too," Annie Sharon said.

"What?" Lucie-Marie asked.

"A spotted calf vest. The chaps to go with it would cost too much, I think."

Cassie said, "Why don't you ask your father before you decide what he'll say."

"Okay, Cassie, I'll try that for a change."

"Yeah, I think we should try that for a change," Lucie-Marie echoed. "Daddy, we need to talk to you before your nap."

chapter 6

"**C**'mon, girls. If you wanna go to this birthday party, we gotta get movin'. I've got a dominoes game set up for myself this afternoon," Tie-Down said impatiently. He loaded Moncado and Tallulah into a horse trailer.

"We're comin', Daddy. We've just finishin' wrappin' Tookie's present."

"Well, get a move on, 'cause I'm leavin' here in five minutes."

Annie Sharon taped the last swirls of ribbon on Tookie's gift, the spotted calf vest they had managed to wrangle Tie-Down into buying.

Lucie Marie watched intently. "That's beautiful,

Annie. Tookie's really gonna like that. It looks like the store did it."

"Think so?" Annie Sharon asked. "We'd better get goin', though. Daddy's not gonna wait for us, and I don't wanna miss any ridin' time with our friends." The girls made their way through the front door.

Tie-Down already sat in the truck, revving the engine. "All right, now. I'll drop you off at Barnes's ranch for the party. Then I'll pick Cassie up and we'll get over to our friend Jake's house. I'm gonna pick you up around seven o'clock. Don't have me looking all over the place for you."

"Absolutely, Daddy, we're gonna have a great time. We're gonna do some bar-be-cuein' and ridin'. That's always fun. Plus, Tookie will open her presents."

Lucie-Marie said, "I know she's gonna like ours. Thanks so much for lettin' us get it. That was so nice of you. You're so good to us, Daddy."

"I try, chile, I try," Tie-Down said softly.

The sun shone hot enough to make the road shimmer, and the breeze did nothing to cool the family as they cruised down Highway 59 toward the ranch with the windows of Tie-Down's truck open. A song by Destiny's Child blared from the radio. Tie-Down really enjoyed his girls when they were laid-back and happy. He experienced none of the squabbling or poked-out mouths he found himself contending with when things were not going to their liking. "Just be good, and be careful on those horses. Have a good time," Tie-Down said.

In unison, the girls responded, "Okay, Daddy."

After a time, the truck pulled up beside a barn at the Triple-R. Annie Sharon and Lucie-Marie almost jumped out of the truck before Tie-Down brought it to a stop.

"Hey, there, Gene. My girls are happy you're havin' a party. Don't let nothin' happen to 'em, now."

"Sho' won't, Tie-Down. My girl insisted on celebratin' her fourteenth birthday with all her friends around. So you best believe I'll be keepin' an eye on 'em."

Tie-Down and the girls went about the task of unloading the horses. Tookie and her guests ran over and set to chattering. Tookie had a head full of crinkly, light blonde hair and deep brown freckles scattered across her face. Her full mouth looked like her father's, but her eyes with their long lashes looked like those of her mother. She giggled a lot and pulled Annie Sharon and Lucie-Marie over to the corral where Diamondback and Black Boo already sat on horseback, along with Rosie M.

Tie-Down's girls waved good-bye to their father as he honked the truck's horn, letting them know he was leaving.

Diamondback, Annie Sharon thought, looked like the musical performer Babyface with a cowboy hat today when he rode toward her. He looked more handsome than usual. Black Boo was the color of the night with no moon, the same as his whole family did when they got off the slave ships, according to his father. That's why he took no offense to his nickname, Black Boo. It was a name he wore and answered to with pride.

All together the friends made up a good-looking bunch. They rarely got into trouble, which endeared them to the adults who kept themselves aware of who their children associated with.

The aroma of roasting beef filled the air, and the teenagers wondered if they could finish their riding before sampling some of the scrumptious food awaiting them. In the end, they decided they would eat when they returned from the ride.

Diamondback checked Lucie-Marie's saddle for her. He did not believe she could handle saddling her own horse. She seemed too small. However, he knew Annie Sharon could be trusted with anything having to do with horses.

Once everyone sat saddled up and ready to go, Tookie led the way to the trail that crisscrossed her father's land. They rode past the apple orchard and made their way through the woods at an easy pace. The cottonwoods hung over them like a halo of small moons. The magnolias and oaks hung low, causing the six of them to watch out for branches and limbs to avoid.

In a short time, Tookie grew restless riding the trail. "C'mon, y'all. Let's head for the open fields where we can race. Nobody'll know the difference."

"But your father might come looking for us," Lucie-Marie warned. "If we change our plans now, he's gonna be pretty upset."

"But it's my birthday. I want to do something exciting like race the guys or ride some broncos. Even wrestle a steer."

"Be sensible, Tookie. Who ever heard of a girl roughhousing a bronc or wrestling a steer?" Diamondback asked.

Annie Sharon and Lucie-Marie both stopped their horses in their tracks. Annie Sharon said, "Our mother could do it. She was an all-around champion."

"That's the truth, too," Lucie-Marie said.

"I'm not doubtin' your mother or disrespectin' her in no way, Annie," Diamondback said. "I'm sorry. I didn't know about this."

Rosie M. broke in. "Well, I think we should go on and have some races, and then go back to the trail. Who's to know? Besides that, I could beat all y'all." Rosie M.'s eyes flashed as she challenged the rest of the group. "Is that really why you don't wanna race us, Diamondback?"

"Aw, you know y'all girls can't beat us," Black Boo said. "We're faster than the wind. Ain't we, Diamondback?"

"Naw, naw, naw," the girls said.

Diamondback stared from one of the girls to the other, shaking his head. The kind of fun he expected to experience this afternoon seemed to be taking a different turn.

"Let's get on to the races; you guys ain't scarin' us none," Annie Sharon said.

Only Lucie-Marie appeared a bit hesitant, but the excitement of the others urged her on. She said to herself, I'm not lettin' anybody get away with doubtin' my mama. And I'm her daughter, so I should be showin' everybody how her blood flows through mine. I'm a champion, too.

Annie Sharon thought the same sort of thing, but with more defiance. *I'm Twanda Rochelle Johnson-Brown's daughter, and somebody thinks they can tell me what girls can and can't do? I don't think so. I'll show 'em.* And off she went to the cleared land on Moncado who must have sensed her energy, because he galloped with fervor from the tree-lined trail to the cleared fields of a pasture.

This led the rest of the group to follow. Annie Sharon was a head or two in front of Rosie M., while Diamondback and Black Boo held back, not believing this challenge they had received from a bunch of girls.

But once they reached the flatlands, they paired off for the races. The field reached out about a mile long, but the distance did not intimidate Annie Sharon or Lucie-Marie. Rosie M. marked a starting place and pointed out a large cactus far off in the distance as the goal.

Rosie M., on her cherished quarter horse Amalia, became the first of the girls to take on one of the boys. Diamondback whispered to her that she would never even make it to the finish.

Rosie M. tried her best to ignore his jibes. Annie Sharon signaled, 'Go,' and the race was on. The girls cheered for Rosie M. while Black Boo sat on his horse laughing until he realized Rosie M. held the lead.

"Darn, Diamondback, how can you let us down this way?" Black Boo did not know this was part of Diamondback's strategy to fool Annie Sharon into believing he was not in good racing form today. He had plans for a later race with Annie Sharon.

Next, Black Boo went up against Lucie-Marie, who sweet-talked Tallulah constantly. "Don't forget, Tallulah, we're doing this for my mama. We've got a tradition to keep up here. Don't you let me down, sweet baby. Not today. Okay?"

Diamondback and Rosie M. returned from the race, and Tookie said, "See there, Diamondback? Y'all ain't all that. Do us proud, Lucie-Marie." This time it was Tookie who gave the signal to start the race.

Annie Sharon shouted, "C'mon, Lucie-Marie. We know you can do it. If we beat them, think how ridiculous they'll look after sayin' girls can't keep up." Annie Sharon gave Diamondback a look that meant he still had her to beat, too, and she had no intention of losing to him.

Lucie-Marie started off slowly, allowing Black Boo to take the lead. She passed him once, then lagged behind again. Annie Sharon grew nervous. She rode after the racers, shouting commands to her sister. "Go on, Lucie-Marie. Tallulah will do whatever you want. Kick her up. You hear me? Use your ridin' crop."

Lucie-Marie did not like using the riding crop

because she thought it made Tallulah too aggressive, but she smacked Tallulah's side on this day. There was too much at stake: boys doubting her and even thinking her incapable of saddling her own horse. Tallulah responded to the riding crop exactly as Lucie-Marie thought she would. She caught up with Black Boo and raced along as if her life depended on her winning this race. Lucie-Marie found herself a little taken aback at the speed at which Tallulah galloped.

She looked back at Black Boo, trailing behind by at least three horse-lengths. She felt herself soaring, riding the clouds. It felt like heaven crossing a wide, green field astride Tallulah. But Lucie-Marie came back to reality when she noticed Black Boo did not intend to give up easily. He closed in on Lucie-Marie by two lengths. But she used her crop again, and Black Boo did not stand a chance.

"Whoa," Lucie said firmly to Tallulah as she rode across the finish ahead of Black Boo by at least four lengths. When they returned to the others, everyone laughed and teased Black Boo about being beat by such a little thing as Lucie-Marie.

"Never mind. That's all right. I'm gonna get mine; you'll see!" Black Boo retorted.

At that moment, Jerome Golightly, another friend of Tookie's, arrived. "Sorry I'm late. I had trouble finding you guys. Tookie, your dad said I'd find y'all on the trail. I had to look all over for you. What's up?"

Tookie considered this her opportunity to win the next race and really take advantage of being the birthday girl.

"C'mon, Jerome. We're racing. Let's go."

"Who? Me and you?" You sure 'bout this?" But, never one to turn down a race, Jerome obliged. He trotted his horse to the starting place Rosie M. pointed out.

Annie Sharon was beside herself, laughing. "You better do somethin' phenomenal, Jerome, because we've beat y'all boys so far. Haven't we, girls?"

The girls clapped and laughed.

Annie Sharon gave the signal for Tookie and Jerome to take off. Away they went across the pasture.

Jerome held his horse back a bit. He did not want Tookie's birthday marred by a loss to him when all of the girls seemed so full of joy. Sure enough, while he pondered the situation in his head, Tookie raced ahead of him and crossed the finish line.

The girls went crazy with excitement: yelling, pointing fingers at the boys, and laughing hard as they struggled to hold each other up.

"How's it feel, guys?" Rosie M. asked, to nobody in particular.

"It was just luck. That's what. Just Pure-D luck," Diamondback answered, not sounding like his usual, cheerful self.

"Yeah," Jerome said, "let's try somethin' harder like, maybe, bronc bustin'? Let's see how you girls do then."

"Oh, I don't think so. That can get danger-ous," Lucie-Marie said.

"Don't let them put you off, Lucie." Annie Sharon pushed her hat back on her head.

"Yeah, we can keep up with y'all at anythin'," Tookie boasted.

"Well, I don't know." Lucie-Marie hesitated.

"Aw, c'mon, Lucie-Marie, I wouldn't let you do anythin' we really shouldn't be doin'," Annie Sharon said.

"Well, are you gonna do it or not?" Black Boo challenged.

"Are we on, girls?" Tookie shouted.

"You bet!" Annie Sharon said.

"Well, all right, then." Jerome snapped his fingers above his head and rode off toward the corral.

The rest of the bunch trotted their horses along behind him, discussing who would go first and who could stay on the wild, bareback broncs for the longest rides.

Declarations of "I'm gonna stay on for the whole eight seconds," and "You ain't gonna make but one second," were followed by "Aw, hush, you don't even know what you're talkin' about."

Once they assembled at the corral, Tookie rode around the barns and stables, making sure her father was nowhere in sight. Something inside warned her the adults would not approve of the crazy thing she and her friends intended to do.

"What you doin'?" Annie Sharon asked Tookie.

"I'm checkin' to see if my pa is around. I'm not sure we should be doin' this. I don't wanna get in trouble on my birthday."

"You won't. We've all been around horses since the time we could crawl. What could go wrong?" Annie Sharon asked. "Let's put our own horses in a corral for now."

Meanwhile, the boys gathered several unbroken horses and set about attaching leather riggings around their bodies for the riders to hold on to. They coaxed the broncs into the chutes for bareback riding. This job proved harder than expected. The wild horses squeezed into the chutes only after a great deal of pulling, and talking, and cajoling. When they were finally in place, they slammed against the sides of the narrow chutes, snorting and kicking.

"Who's got a watch?" Jerome asked when the horses quieted a bit.

A chorus of "I do's" filled the air, but the question remained unanswered as to who would go first. Finally, Tookie pulled a coin from a pocket of her jeans. She told Annie Sharon and Diamondback to call heads or tails as she tossed the coin into the air. Diamond-back called heads and won the toss. He became the first rider.

Jerome stationed himself in the arena to assist the tossed riders while Black Boo made himself ready to distract the angry horses once the riders were thrown.

Diamondback climbed into position and balanced himself on the sides of the wooden chute. He eased himself onto the bronco's back. His left fist closed around the rigging and he announced he was ready.

When the gate of the chute flew open, Diamondback shot off on the back of a horse that definitely did not want him there. Tookie kept her eyes on the second hand of her watch while Diamondback hung onto the rigging with his left hand. He kept his right hand extended high in the air above his head. When he used the spurs on his boots to agitate the horse, his ride grew as dangerous as Lucie-Marie predicted it might be. Diamondback hung on for six long seconds before his body slammed onto the soft dirt of Gene Barnes's Arena Number Two.

Jerome picked Diamondback up and dusted him off, praising him all the while for his awesome ride.

Annie Sharon declared herself the next bronc buster. She straddled the chute waiting for its gate to open. She coached herself while she wrapped a hand around the rigging on the back of the horse. The gate flew open, and the horse bounded out, bucking for all he was worth. Annie Sharon spurred him on, and would not let go, even when Tookie shouted to her, "Let go! You made eight seconds, girl. Annie Sharon, you gonna get hurt!"

Annie Sharon seemed possessed by a force greater than she. She imagined her mother out there with her. She could not let go of the horse until this spirit let go of her and, right now, the spirit held her captive. The unbroken horse bucked furiously, trying to rid himself of his unwanted rider. The longer Annie Sharon hung on, the angrier the horse became. But suddenly Annie Sharon felt herself lifted off the back of the animal by a large, strong hand that grabbed the belt of her jeans and held her in its grasp.

Out of nowhere, Tie-Down was back early, and in the nick of time to save his daughter from her own folly. He helped her scramble onto the back of his horse.

Tookie's father, who brought Tie-Down with him to check on the youngsters, rode to help Black Boo chase the bronc back to a chute and out of the arena. But the horse ran about wildly, snorting and kicking up its heels.

Tie-Down allowed Annie Sharon to slide from his horse to the ground. He leaped down after her. Without asking questions or saying a word, Tie-Down slapped Annie Sharon hard across her face with his open palm. Twice.

Annie Sharon staggered backward, a hand darting to her cheek, her eyes watering and glaring wide, revealing her shock, disbelief, and pain.

"Are you trying to kill yourself? You don't know nothin' about bronc ridin'. Why do you keep doing these fool things?"

Cassie entered the arena through an empty chute in time to see Tie-Down slap his daughter. She found it hard to believe he still resorted to hitting after her discussion with him about abuse. As she ran to console Annie Sharon, the thrashing young horse crashed against Tie-Down. He knocked him to the ground, leaving him dazed and disoriented.

Gene Barnes and Black Boo ran toward Tie-Down to distract the horse. They did not reach Tie-Down in time. The two of them watched helplessly as the horse arched its back, sprang high in the air, and landed on its front feet. It kicked high with its hind feet. As the small crowd watched in horror, the horse's hind feet slammed down against the side of Tie-Down's head.

Tie-Down lay motionless in the dirt for a few seconds before screams escaped the girls' lips and the young men ran to help Black Boo and Gene Barnes handle the horse. Annie Sharon fell onto the ground, sobbing and begging Tie-Down to speak to her. The others gathered around. Cassie scrambled into the midst of the crowd surrounding Tie-Down. She pushed and shoved them away, demanding he be given space and air.

"Call 911, somebody," Cassie yelled as her practiced hands darted between Tie-Down's neck and a wrist, checking for pulses. Her hair fell onto his face as she jammed her face close to his, praying for a whisper of breath.

As if released from a mute, frozen state, everyone suddenly shouted questions at

Cassie. She sat back on her heels, her eyes roving past each of the young faces surrounding her. "I don't know," she said. "Did somebody call an ambulance? This can't be happening, not after we've decided to get married and be together forever." Her voice was a whisper, barely heard above the sobs and the promises that everyone in the arena knew they might be making too late.

Lucie-Marie sat on the edge of Tie-Down's hospital bed, holding his hand in hers. She smiled at him and asked, "How long will you have that bandage plastered to the side of your head?"

Tie-Down replied, "A better question is how long it's gonna take for my hair to grow back in."

Cassie laughed. She sat in the large recliner that filled a corner of the room. She glanced at Annie Sharon, who sat on a straight wooden chair across the room in another corner. Cassie pondered what she should say to the girl.

Annie Sharon's back was pressed against the back of the chair. She sat erect, staring out of a window. Her face was twisted into a frown, and it seemed obvious she did not want to be a part of the light conversation and banter in the room. Her hands were scrunched together into a tight ball, which rested in her lap.

Cassie caught Tie-Down's eye and nodded her head slightly in the direction of Annie Sharon.

Tie-Down cleared his throat. "All right, girls. Let's talk about the big problem that's looming before us here. Cassie tells me that y'all know that me and her have been talking marriage. I hadn't mentioned it to you 'cause it wasn't somethin' we were sure of yet ourselves. The other night, we just tossed the notion around. Sort of, 'What if?'" He looked at Annie Sharon to see how this announcement was going over with her.

Annie Sharon continued to gaze through the window as if spellbound by something of great importance outside.

"Annie Sharon," Tie-Down said. "We were gonna discuss this with you. We can't hook up and have the kind of life we want if you two ain't gonna be happy, too. We wouldn't do this unless y'all are in agreement. I love Cassie. I'm sure y'all know that by now. But you're my daughters, and you know I loved you first. I always will, with all my heart."

Lucie-Marie said, "Daddy, we know that. And we pretty much knew you loved Cassie, too. But you have to talk to us; we're not little kids anymore. We can understand this kinda stuff. Can't we, Annie Sharon?"

Annie Sharon turned to look at the three other people in the room. Her eyes came to rest on her father. "It's just been the three of us for almost as long as I can remember. I like us the way we are. I learned to cook so I could make our food. Lucie-Marie learned to use the washer so she could keep our clothes clean. Dupree stepped in to help teach us 'bout horses. It's been hard, but we made it work. Then Cassie showed up." Annie Sharon's eyes moved to Cassie again. "It's not that I don't like you, but . . ." Her voice trailed off.

"I know," Cassie said. "I'm like an extra wheel, like an intruder. Girls, I don't want to be. For a long time, I didn't even know I was falling in love with your daddy; we're such different people. I just knew I kept being drawn back to him. And though I've never been a mother, I felt myself coming to care deeply for you girls, too. And I want to make a relationship with you."

Tie-Down broke in. "There's too much love here for us to just let it go by the wayside. When I get out of here, let's sit down and have a serious talk—see where we're all at. I promise you, me and Cassie won't keep secrets from you. But, then, you'll have to talk to us, too. Even about things that are hard. Are we all agreed on that?"

The others nodded.

Annie Sharon stared at Cassie for a time. "Cassie," she said, "I don't know what would've happened if you hadn't shown up at the Barneses' ranch when you did. Daddy was right; what we did was a fool thing. And the only one of us thinkin' straight was Lucie-Marie. She tol' us it was dangerous. And look what happened—we almost lost our daddy."

"Well, you didn't," Tie-Down said. "When we

get outta here, we're gonna all make some changes."

"When will we GET outta here?" Lucie-Marie asked.

"Well, the doctors just keep takin' X rays, over and over. We can't go till they're all agreed it's time. And they said I might as well forget the rest of this season; they ain't gonna give me an okay to compete."

"They don't take chances, Tie-Down," Cassie said. "But we could just take you on home today, and I could use the Tarot to speculate how you're gonna come along."

"Oh, no," Tie-Down said. "If you'll promise not to read cards at me, I'll promise to stay here as long as I need to."

"It's going to be a long, slow summer," Cassie said. "We can all just hang loose and get to know each other better. Uh-oh. It seems like I'm the only one who'll have to work. I think I'm jealous of the rest of you."

"We'll have to help Dupree keep the ranch going," Annie Sharon said. "He still has to be careful of his ribs, too."

"We can do that," Lucie Marie said.

"Come here, all of y'all," Tie-Down said.

Minutes later a nurse came into the room with pills for Tie-Down. She stopped in her tracks when she saw four people in his bed, laughing and hugging each other. "Seems like our rooms need more chairs," the nurse said.

"Oh, you got enough chairs," Tie-Down said. "I just like havin' all the girls I love around me."